Pick of the Litter

BILL WALLACE

Pick
of the
Litter

ALADDIN PAPERBACKS

NEW YORK   LONDON   TORONTO   SYDNEY

In memory of
J. C.,
who shared so much love with all of us

ALADDIN PAPERBACKS
An imprint of Simon & Schuster Children's Publishing Division
1230 Avenue of the Americas, New York, NY 10020
Copyright © 2005 by Bill Wallace
All rights reserved, including the right of reproduction in whole or in part in any form.
Published by arrangement with Holiday House
For information, contact Holiday House, 475 Madison Avenue, New York, New York 10017.
ALADDIN PAPERBACKS and colophon are trademarks of Simon & Schuster, Inc.
Manufactured in the United States of America
First Aladdin Paperbacks edition June 2006
2 4 6 8 10 9 7 5 3
The Library of Congress has cataloged the hardcover edition as follows:
Wallace, Bill, 1947–
Pick of the litter / by Bill Wallace.—1st ed.
p. cm.
Summary: Twelve-year-old Tom learns first-hand about honor, first when he is wrongly accused of lying at school, then when he faces the risk of losing a puppy he has come to love while helping his grandfather train hunting dogs, but writing to a new friend helps him sort his feelings and do the right thing.
ISBN: 0-8234-1921-5 (hc)
[1. Conduct of life—Fiction. 2. Pointer (Dog breed)—Fiction. 3. Dogs—Training—Fiction.
4. Grandfathers—Fiction. 5. Letters—Fiction.] I. Title.
PZ7.W15473Pi 2005
[Fic]—dc22   2004052321
ISBN-13: 978-1-4169-2511-8 (pbk)
ISBN-10: 1-4169-2511-2 (pbk)

 Chapter 1

My eyes were so tight and hot, the paper in front of me looked red. When I glared at the two columns of gray words, my vision blurred, and the lines squiggled and zigzagged down the page.

I didn't like spelling. No—I take that back.

I *hated* spelling!

What I wanted to do was rip the papers to shreds, storm out the door, and not come back. I could tell Mama I was sick. If that didn't work—what could my teacher do? Send me to the office? Big deal! Mrs. Bowlin never did anything. She probably wouldn't even be there.

Another puff of red clouded my vision when I glanced up from my paper to the window. Kids were still on the playground, but Danny and Mark weren't around—they were headed to the creek to look for frogs and snakes. They were probably already there, finding all sorts of neat stuff.

Not me. I was stuck in the teachers' lounge. All alone. Writing spelling words I missed on the test.

Why would *anyone* have a spelling test on the last Wednesday of school? Nobody had tests the last week of school. It was ridiculous! Stupid.

I hated spelling.

I clutched my pencil in my hand like a dagger.

"I'd like to . . . ," I muttered. Then I turned the pencil back the way it was supposed to be. If I stabbed the paper, I'd just break my lead and have to go sharpen it again. I wrote the word "persuade" at the top of the third column.

"*U*," I snarled to myself. "Not *W*, you dummy!"

Then I wrote it again, right under the first "persuade."

But what I hated even more than spelling was having to write the words—in cursive. I hated *that* more than chicken pox. More than poison ivy.

Mrs. Dunn made us learn cursive in third grade, but when it came to a spelling test we could either write or print. In fourth grade, Mrs. Cooperton made us use cursive. But when we had to write the words we missed, she would accept them either way. With Mrs. Nash . . . we didn't have a choice.

I could remember, back in the old days, when printing was a lot faster. I could do one column of *p*, go back to the top and scamper down with *e*, then back up, and do the *rs*'s. With cursive, I had to write the whole, stinking word. No short-cuts. Just "persuade," "persuade," "persuade," "persuade" . . . until I was so sick of it I could barf.

I ought to go home, I thought. *Why not? The worst that could happen was miss recess tomor-row. I could sneak off and—*

My head snapped up. The sound of the door-knob rattling yanked my eyes from the window, back to the page.

Footsteps.

Probably one of the teachers coming in to get something from the pop machine.

No. The clopping shoes came closer. They stopped right behind me.

"Almost done?" Mrs. Nash's voice made me want to turn and look up at her. I didn't. I just kept writing "persuade," over and over and over again.

She stood there, for a long time, without a word. Finally she moved beside me, turned, and leaned against the edge of the table. She didn't sit on it or my paper, but she was so close, I couldn't get my elbow up there to write. When I realized I couldn't avoid her any longer, I put my pencil down and looked up.

Mrs. Nash's eyebrows arched. "I'm sorry you're mad at me," she began.

All right, I guess I didn't *look up* at her— maybe it was more like a glare.

"But . . . ," she went on, "staying after school to write your spelling words really wasn't my idea. It was *yours*."

My mouth flopped open so wide, my chin almost bumped the table. I snapped my mouth shut and kept it shut.

Mrs. Nash held her school bag in her lap. She reached in, pulled out her grade book, and ran her finger down the page.

"First nine weeks, you struggled a little. Either you didn't know how to study your spelling words, or you didn't take the time to learn them." She flipped the page. "Second nine weeks, you did really well. Only missed two words, right before Christmas vacation"—she turned another page—"and two more right before spring break." She flipped the last page.

"Then you quit!"

I looked up at her, but for only an instant before I turned my eyes away.

"Not only did you quit, but two weeks ago"— she tapped her finger on the page—"you missed five and you didn't turn in your spelling words the next day. I let that one slide. I knew you were worried about your grandfather, and there was a lot going on. But last week you missed two words. I was willing to forget that, too. I know your grandfather was scheduled for surgery on the day after the test. However . . ." She took a breath. "Thursday morning, you told me your paper was in your backpack, but you couldn't find it. You promised you'd keep looking. And?" she asked.

I kept my eyes on the page.

"And?" she repeated.

When I still didn't say anything, she answered herself. "And you spent every spare minute you had, writing the spelling words that you *told me you did* Wednesday. Right?"

"Yes, ma'am."

She sat quietly for a long time. Finally she leaned down, and made me look at her.

"You remember how we've talked about honor?"

"Yes, ma'am."

"Do you remember what honor means?"

"Yes, ma'am. It means doing what's right. Not fighting on the playground, not telling lies, not cheating on a test, and . . . you know . . . stuff like that."

"It means a lot more, Tom. It also means trust. Trust and honor are both forms of respect. You're not on your honor just during school, or when you're taking a test. You're on your honor every day. And Tom . . ."

She made me look at her.

". . . it's not for me, but for *you*. You know what's right—what's honest. You do it, not because someone might catch you, but because it's the right thing to do." She paused. "When you finish, leave your paper right here on the table. I'll pick it up in the morning." She stood and walked across the room. At the door, she hesitated. "Your mom is waiting in the west parking lot. See you tomorrow."

I sat there for a long time. Even though it made me mad to miss going to the creek with my friends, I knew Mrs. Nash was right. I did lie to her. Last week I told her I had done my spelling when I hadn't. This week I figured, since it was the end of school, she wouldn't bother. I'd lied to her. Not just once but . . .

I wrote the word "persuade" again, then again, then again, then . . .

Between "bureau," "tournament," and "persuade," I ran out of room on the first page. "Quotient" and "variety" took two columns on a second piece of paper.

When I finally finished, I left the papers, hopped up, raced down the hall, out the front door, and around the side of the school. As I came into view of the parking lot, I slowed down and let my shoulders slump. Trudged slowly, almost painfully, toward Mama's car.

Racing to the car wouldn't work. Maybe if I looked sad and remorseful enough, she wouldn't be so tough on me.

Mama never said a word. Not on the way home. Not during supper, not even the next morning when she drove me to school.

In a way, I wish she had. I wish she'd yelled at me, or told Daddy what I did. Or grounded me. Something. Anything!

Not saying one single word made me feel terrible. I didn't think anything could make me feel worse.

At least, that's what I *thought* . . . until Mrs. Nash finished taking attendance and lunch count on Friday morning.

She closed her grade book, stood up, and smoothed down the front of her dress. Then very softly—almost a whisper—she said:

"Thomas. I need to see you in the hall."

Chapter 2

The instant Mrs. Nash closed the door, she wheeled on me. Glaring down with her fists on her hips, she leaned so close that her nose almost touched mine.

"Thomas, until the last three weeks, you have been one of my best students, honest and dependable. I don't have to worry about your getting in trouble on the playground, or cheating on tests.

"But what you did yesterday afternoon was *totally* unacceptable!"

I felt my mouth fall open. I wanted to ask what I did, but she didn't give me the chance.

"You were to finish your spelling words *before* you went home. Not take them with you to work on. You were to stay and then leave them on the table. Go get them—right now!"

Somehow, I managed to force my mouth to work.

"I . . . I . . . but I . . ." Even with my lips moving, I still couldn't talk. All I could do was stammer. Mrs. Nash sighed.

"I never *ever* dreamed I could be so disappointed in you. Even if it *is* the last day of school, I fully intend to call your mother and father in for a conference. I cannot believe you did that."

"Did what?" I gasped, finally.

Mrs. Nash hovered over me. Looking straight up, all I could see was her chin, and her eyes glaring down from beneath her glasses.

"You left without finishing your spelling words."

"I—I finished them, Mrs. Nash."

"Then where are they?"

My arms shook. My legs trembled. My mouth flopped, but no words came out. All I could do was point down the hall toward the teachers' lounge.

Mrs. Nash stomped off. After a few paces, she realized I wasn't following. She turned and crooked her finger. My legs were shaking so hard I didn't know if they'd hold me up. Almost staggering, I followed.

This couldn't be happening. I *did* my words. All five of them. Twenty-five times, each. I even counted them, twice, just to make sure. I left them on the table, like she told me.

It was a dream.

It had to be a bad dream. I was still in my bed, at home. In a second I'd wake up and . . . and . . .

And Mrs. Nash opened the door to the teachers' lounge. Holding it wide open, she made a swooping motion with her arm for me to go in.

Maybe it wasn't a dream.

Come on, I urged. *Wake up. Open your eyes.*

There was the table—TOTALLY EMPTY!

This wasn't a nightmare. I was awake.

"Where are your spelling words, Tom?"

My finger shook when I pointed at the table. Then it curled into a fist, with the rest of my fingers. My arms shook at my side. My knees trembled. Suddenly, I felt dizzy.

"Right there, Mrs. Nash." The words whooshed out of me like a gust of wind. But when I sucked in another breath, I didn't feel dizzy anymore. "I left them right there on the table."

"They're not there now."

I stared at the empty tabletop.

"Did you tell your mother you were done and run off to play with your friends? Are they in your backpack, finished? Or did you simply stop the second I left the building, not write another word, and plan to finish them during class?"

I shook my head.

"Go back to the room and get your spelling words, Tom. Let me see how much you have done."

Don't hold your breath, I told myself, forcing in another gulp of air. *You'll end up flat on your face if you don't keep breathing.* I felt my nostrils clamp together as I struggled to let the air out slowly.

"They were right there," I whispered. "I swear, Mrs. Nash. I finished all . . ." Pausing, I heard a gulping sound when I swallowed. ". . . of them. They were right there. I promise!"

For a long time she stood, looking down at me. I could see the expression on her face, and I could tell she still didn't believe me.

The longer we stood there, the worse I felt. My fists were so tight, my fingernails dug into my palms. My knees locked—muscles straining until I could feel myself shaking all over. And I hurt. Not a hurt like scraping my knee on the sidewalk or getting tackled in football and landing on my shoulder. The hurt was deeper. It was clear down in the pit of my stomach.

A hurt that gnawed on my insides, because I *was* telling her the truth—only she didn't (or couldn't) believe me.

I guess she was waiting for me to "break." Waiting for me to tell her the truth. Waiting for me to go back to the room and get my half-finished list of spelling words out of my backpack.

But I couldn't. I *had* told her the truth. There was nothing more I could do.

"Let's go back to the room," she said, finally.

We were almost out the door when Mrs. Nash stopped. I dodged to get out of her way, but she still bumped into me. "Sorry," she said as she walked to the far side of the teachers' lounge. I stood and watched. In the corner, she leaned over and picked up the trash can. She looked inside, then set it down. Her eyes seemed to scan every part of the room as she turned.

There was a bookshelf on the wall beside the pop machine. She walked to it, looked on each shelf, even felt above the books with her hand. She looked behind the little table where the coffeepot was, and behind the pop machine. Finally her gaze fell on me.

"Go on, Tom. I'll be down there in a second."

"May I stop by the restroom?"

She nodded.

I didn't need to go. I just needed a couple of minutes to quit shaking. Everybody knew something was going on—something was wrong.

She wants to believe me, I thought as I washed my hands at the sink. I glanced at the mirror. The face that looked back at me wasn't a very nice face. It was the face of a liar.

How could Mrs. Nash believe me? I'd lied to her about forgetting my spelling words. She'd trusted me, and I'd lied to her. Even if she wanted to believe me—even though I *was* telling the truth—how could she now?

Why would she even try?

 Chapter 3

Friday was the longest day I ever spent in my entire life!

Mrs. Nash didn't say anything when I came back to the room. None of the guys tried to ask what was going on, either. Although I tried my best to look calm and relaxed, everybody could probably tell I was upset.

Mrs. Nash gathered up our social studies, math, and science texts. Then she let people go, one at a time, to return any library books that they had forgotten to bring back.

When Carl Decker went, Mrs. Nash followed him to the door. She had good cause to keep an eye on Carl. He was one of those guys who was always doing stuff he wasn't supposed to.

I couldn't help wondering if I was "one of those guys" now. I didn't *think* I was. But I'd given Mrs. Nash more than enough cause to feel that way about me. From now on, she'd probably watch me like she did Carl. Keep an eye on him until he got where he was headed, then come back to work with us.

Only today, as soon as Carl had time to make it to the library, Mrs. Nash slipped out the door.

The pencil sharpener was on the doorjamb. I found a pencil and went to sharpen it. When I leaned to peek around the corner, Mrs. Nash was no place in sight.

Ms. Lee's room was right across from ours. Her door opened. Mrs. Nash backed out, said "Thank you," then trotted next door to Mr. Marcum's class. I kept sharpening the pencil. Finally she went to Mrs. Meyer's room.

I glanced at my pencil. It was just about down to the nub, so I scampered to my seat. I timed it perfectly, because she came back a second or two after I plopped into my chair.

When Harry Croft went to take his library books, she did the same thing she'd done before.

Harry was always getting into stuff, just like Carl—only worse. Harry was mean. He was always trying to bully people. She waited by the door a moment or two, then slipped out and went in the other direction. My timing was a little off. When she came out of Miss McMaster's room, I was watching under my left elbow. I pretty much knew she saw me, because nobody sticks their elbow in the air and leans under it while they're sharpening a pencil.

Instead of trying to make it to my desk, I just kept grinding.

Mrs. Nash paused at the door and turned like she was watching for Harry.

"That pencil is almost down to the eraser." She whispered so none of the other kids could hear. "Go sit."

Sitting was next to impossible. I wiggled, squirmed, shifted my weight from one cheek to the other. I wondered if she'd already called Mama and Daddy. I wondered if she was waiting for Mrs. Bowlin to come and take me to the office.

I didn't know what was going to happen to me. The not knowing made every breath stick in my throat. It forced all thoughts of summer, and playing with my friends, clear to the back of my head—to a dark, sinister place, where I couldn't even dream about fun. All I could see was trouble. Disaster.

At morning recess, Danny and Mark came tearing up to me. "What happened, Tom?" The two voices sounded together like a yell that echoed across the playground.

I shushed them.

"Nothing," I lied.

Four eyes stared at me.

"Okay," I confessed. "I missed some words on my spelling test, but I didn't write them and turn them in on Thursday morning. Mrs. Nash made me stay after school to finish them."

Mark scratched his nose. "We wondered why you didn't show up at the creek yesterday."

Danny kind of shoved him aside with an elbow. "Yeah, but why were you shaking so hard when you came back to the room? Why were you so upset?"

"She can't find my papers."

Mark tilted his head to the side. "Did you really do them?"

Danny and I both glared at him.

Taking a step back, he gave a little shrug. "Just asking."

Danny looked over his shoulder. "Bet Carl or Harry got them. Sounds like something those two would do. Soon as we get back in the room, I'll check Carl's desk. Mark, you take a peek in Harry's and—"

"No," I said, cutting him off. "I was in the teachers' lounge. I left them on the—"

"The teachers' lounge?" Mark yelped. "You mean you really got to go in there? What's it like? Do they have soft couches? Recliners? A big-screen TV? Do they really have an electric paddle? Daddy always told me they did—you know—back in the old days. Did they have it stored in there? What does it look like? Were there any—"

"Mark!" Danny snarled. "Shut! Up! Tom's in trouble and you're flapping your lips like a complete dork." He turned back to me. "Did you look on the floor? Maybe they fell off and . . ."

I shook my head. "They weren't on the floor."

"How about the trash can? Maybe somebody threw them away and . . ."

I shook my head again. "Mrs. Nash looked there. She looked behind the coffeepot, the pop machine, she even felt around on top of the books on the tall bookshelf. No spelling papers."

"Maybe somebody threw them out in the trash," Mark suggested. "At noon recess, we could dig around in the Dumpsters."

Danny rolled his eyes. "Mark, every teacher in the building dumps paper and trash on the last day of school. It'd be like trying to find a flea on an elephant's butt."

"Well." Mark held his hands up. "We might get lucky."

Danny just stared at him. Finally, Mark shrugged and offered a halfhearted smile. "I'm gonna go play softball. See ya later."

With that he sprinted off across the playground.

Morning recess was a little longer than usual, but I couldn't enjoy it. When we got back in, Mrs.

Nash handed out art paper and we got to draw and visit for a while—"As long as we kept the noise down."

Still nervous and shaky, the two pictures I drew were terrible. I kept glancing at my teacher. She watched the clock on our wall.

What was she going to do to me? And WHEN was she going to do it?

Not finding the papers that I *really* did was bad enough. But what was worse was Mrs. Nash didn't believe me. That hurt. I liked Mrs. Nash. She was the best teacher I'd ever had. She'd never trust me again. Just the thought made me feel like dirt. No, I felt lower than dirt.

All of a sudden, she sort of hopped up from her desk and trotted to the door.

"I'm going to be out of the room for a moment," she announced. "I want you to stay in your seats, and I want all visiting to stop until I get back. And I mean *all*. Samantha, take names at the chalkboard. When I get back, if there is a name up there, that person will be the *last* to leave the room on the *last day* of school." Her gaze seemed to drift to Carl Decker's side of the room. "And if anyone threatens Samantha for putting his name on the board—that person will wait with me, *after school,* until every single person in the entire building has gone home."

This was it. Mama and Daddy were probably waiting for her in the office. I was dead. The whole summer would be shot. I'd be grounded until school started next year.

I began to put a smile on the face I was drawing on my art paper.

I hadn't even finished drawing it, when my own smile vanished and a knot came up in my throat.

It took forever for Mrs. Nash to come back. When I heard the door open, my heart skipped a beat. She stood in the doorway for a second, then . . .

"Thomas Danfield," she called. "I have something to say to you."

My heart stopped.

Slowly. Every eye in the room. Turned. Toward. Me.

This was it! I was dead.

I wanted *not* to be here. I wished I could vanish. Suddenly appear somewhere else.

If I were only small enough to slink under my desk and hide there, never to be seen again. If only . . .

Chapter 4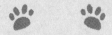

"Tom," she repeated as she started across the room. "I owe you an apology."

My head snapped up.

"I made you stay after school yesterday to write your spelling words. When I couldn't find them this morning, I accused you of taking them home, or not even doing them.

"I was wrong!"

My eyes flashed.

She walked slowly, speaking each word softly yet loud enough so everyone could hear. She crossed the front of the room and paused at my row.

"When I confronted you and threatened to call your parents, you swore that you had done your work. I didn't believe you. But you were so sincere, I decided to ask the teachers if anyone had seen them."

She was almost to my chair now.

"Not one single teacher, secretary, not even the principal had seen them." She stood, towering above me, leaning forward with her arms behind her.

"Mr. Clark comes in at ten forty-five, to set up the lunch tables. I asked him." She brought her arms from behind her back. In her right hand were two sheets of paper. They were folded, kind of sloppy and crooked, but the instant she opened them . . .

"He cleaned the lounge yesterday afternoon. The papers were in his way, but he couldn't tell if they were important or not, so instead of throwing them in the trash, he folded them and stuck them on top of the bookshelf. They were back from the edge, where neither you nor I could see them." She folded the papers, then dropped to one knee beside my desk.

"I really am sorry," she whispered, so no one

else could hear. Her soft, gentle hands forced the folded papers into my grasp. "You're a good and honest young man. I should have believed you."

As I looked at her eyes, I heard the words—not from her mouth—but straight from her heart.

A little chill shot across my back and shoulders. The kind that races up your neck and around your head to tug at your eyes. For the first time since I was little, I felt like crying. I didn't, but I couldn't say anything, either. All I could do was smile at her, and nod my head.

We got an extra-long lunch recess. That was fun. Once back in our room, Mrs. Nash read the last two chapters of *Stubby and the Puppy Pack: To the Rescue.*

The fact that we kept pestering her to finish the book probably had something to do with it. I was glad she did. There was a part of me that kind of hoped Stubby and the dogs would leave that nasty Kylie stuck in the hole. But they were nice, and that wouldn't be a very nice thing to do. I liked the way it ended.

By the time she was done, we were a lot quieter than we had been when we first came in from the playground. She had us all clean out our desks and put our personal things like pencils, extra notebook paper, and junk into our backpacks.

Terri and Debra volunteered to clean out the big cardboard box where we kept our playground balls, baseballs, and bats. Some people had been using the box like a trash can—there was so much paper in the bottom, we had to dig to find anything to play with.

They dragged the huge box up beside the front door, so it was closer to the trash can. When the can was full, Mrs. Nash picked me to take it out. I chose Danny to help.

"That was totally awesome this morning," Danny said when we opened the Dumpster.

"What was?" I asked, lifting the trash can to the edge and pouring the paper in.

"The way Mrs. Nash apologized to you. I mean, I never heard a teacher apologize to a kid before. What was she doing when she got down on one knee?"

"She gave my papers back to me."

"She said something." Danny arched an eyebrow. "What did she say?"

I didn't answer him. I never told anyone what Mrs. Nash said to me.

When we got back, Terri and Debra had the box tipped over on its side so Terri could crawl in and dig out the paper. About halfway in the box, she kind of looked like a dog digging for a bone. She scraped paper beside herself, between her legs, and even tossed some over her shoulders. Debra grabbed what she raked out and started stuffing it into the trash can that we just set down.

The can was almost full again when Mrs. Bowlin popped in.

She always showed up on the last day of school to give her end-of-the-year speech.

First she would tell everyone what a good year it had been. Then she'd warn us that, just because it was the last day of school, we shouldn't get too excited and forget to watch for cars on our way home. Finally she'd give us a big smile and tell all of us to have a fun summer.

Right as she walked through the doorway, she opened her mouth to start her speech. Then she glanced down. I guess—from where she stood—

all she could see was Terri's bottom sticking out of the big box.

She blinked a couple of times, turned to Mrs. Nash, and grinned.

"Cleaning the room before summer vacation is always appreciated," she said. "But don't you think that throwing away a perfectly good student is a little much?"

Mrs. Nash put both fists on her hips and shot Mrs. Bowlin an irritated look—the same look we got when we were too noisy or someone acted smart-alecky with her. Mrs. Bowlin clamped her lips together, spun, and was out of the room before Terri could back out of the box.

"Who was that?" Terri asked. "What's going on?"

Suddenly Mrs. Bowlin leaned her head back inside. I guess she remembered why she'd come to our room in the first place.

"Hope all of you have a good summer!" she yelled, still grinning.

"Thank you," we called back.

Danny and I hauled another load of trash to the Dumpster. The thing was so full, Danny had to climb in and jump up and down to pack the paper enough so we could close the lid. Bob Evans and Randall Jenkins brought a pile of trash from their room.

"You two gonna be on our baseball team this summer?" Bob asked.

"Don't know." Danny grinned. "I heard you were gonna be the pitcher. I didn't think you could even get the ball across the plate."

He punched Bob on the shoulder. Bob shoved him back, and they both started laughing and scuffling.

I looked at them, then turned and headed for the building.

 Chapter 5

Everyone was seated. Hands folded on the desk-tops and sitting up straight, they all watched our teacher. As soon as I put down the trash can, she motioned me to my chair. Keeping her eyes on the door, Mrs. Nash stood for a moment until Danny came in and sat down. Clearing her throat, she smiled. "I am pretty sure most of you already know this, but next year our school system is start-ing what they call 'tracking.' This means that a teacher will start with a class in third grade and stay with that same class every year until the stu-dents finish sixth grade, and move to junior high.

"What it means to you, specifically, is that I will be your teacher again next year."

She had to stop talking, because some of the girls started clapping. All of us joined in.

Well . . . all except Carl and Harry. The rest of us liked Mrs. Nash and were glad that she was going to be our teacher again next year. They didn't. Of course, they didn't like Mrs. Parks from first grade or Mrs. Dunn from third grade, either. That's probably because they didn't like anyone who expected them to mind. So we just ignored them and clapped even harder.

Mrs. Nash glanced at the clock and held up her hands to get us quiet.

"I'm looking forward to having each of you again. There is a lot more reading in sixth grade, so I hope you will find some time to read this summer. We'll also do a lot more work on our writing skills next year. Keeping a journal over the summer or writing letters will help maintain the skills you already have and improve them for next school year."

Better write that down, I thought. I grabbed my spelling papers from my backpack and scribbled: Writing skills. Journal. Letters.

The bell rang!

I couldn't believe it. I had all but given up on ever getting out of school for summer. We all started grabbing stuff and leaping to our feet.

"Stop!"

We stopped.

"Sit down!"

Not too quiet, we shuffled back into our chairs. The bell had stopped ringing by the time we were settled.

"Read some and write some!" Then Mrs. Nash's face softened to a gentle smile. "And have a fun summer. Samantha's row."

My row was next to last. Once we were all waiting in line at the door, Mrs. Nash told us to watch for cars and to play safe. Then she let us go. Some of the girls stopped to give her a quick hug. I acted like I was trying to find something in my backpack. The people behind me went on around. Once everyone was out of the room, I gave Mrs. Nash a hug, too.

"It wasn't your fault," I told her. "If I had done my words, like I was supposed to . . . well . . . it was *my* fault."

Mrs. Nash hugged me back. "I'm glad you're going to be in my room next year." She smiled.

"Me too."

I took off to catch up with my class.

"Don't run in the halls!" she called, loud enough so we could hear her over all the commotion.

Mama always parked near the front of the car line, but I didn't see her when I got outside. Not that I thought much about it. Lots of parents picked up their kids on the last day of school, because they had so much stuff to lug around. She was probably someplace at the back of the line.

I walked down a ways. When I still didn't spot our car, I sat on the benches near the front door.

Checking to make sure no one was watching, I opened my backpack just enough to slip my hand inside and pull out the two sheets of paper with my spelling words on them.

You're not on your honor just during school, or when you're taking a test. Mrs. Nash's words rattled inside my head, when I stared at the words I'd written. *You know what's right—what's honest. You do it, not because someone might catch you, but because it's the right thing to do.*

"Tom."

Mrs. Nash's voice made my head snap up. I stuffed the pages back in my pack.

"Yes, ma'am?"

"Your mother is parked out on the road. Weren't you supposed to go someplace today?"

Suddenly remembering, I hopped to my feet and trotted toward her.

"Yes, ma'am," I said. "My grandfather just got home from the hospital. Mama and I are going to help feed the dogs and clean the kennels until he's feeling better."

She held up a hand, stopping the car that was trying to pull around us. I scurried across the drive.

With all that had happened the last couple of days—mad because I had to write spelling words, guilty because I lied to Mrs. Nash, scared because we couldn't find my papers, humiliated because I couldn't hide how upset it made me, proud when she called me "an honorable young man"—all those feelings mixed up and jumbled together and all flying at me—all at once . . .

I was more than ready for summer. I wanted to tell Mama everything that had happened. I wanted to see how Grandpa was feeling. I could hardly wait to run and play and go fishing. I was dying to kick off my shoes and run around barefoot. I longed for the sweet smell of summer.

Chapter 6

When longing for the sweet smell of summer, a dog kennel isn't exactly the place to hang out.

"Mama. It stinks!"

"What did you expect?" She offered a half-hearted smile. "There are thirty-six dogs and twenty-eight pens. That's not even counting the puppies. Your grandmother's done a fabulous job. Two weeks ago, when your grandfather had his heart attack, she rushed him to the hospital, and stayed with him. Your father took the day off from his job to be here and clean kennels and feed. After they got him stabilized—you know—when your grandfather wasn't in danger, they did two days of testing. She got up before daylight, came out with the flashlight to feed, then rushed to the hospital so she could be there with him. Same thing in the evenings.

"Your dad and I helped cleaned the pens. But since we don't know the names, we couldn't let them out to run or go poop—they could only go to their outside runs."

"Know the names?" I asked.

"Your grandfather trains his dogs to respond to their names—he calls them by name then gives a command, like 'come' or 'sit' . . . you know? How he remembers all of them, I have no idea. But your grandmother only knows some. That's fine, though. Except for these six in the old milk barn, they all have outside runs. They don't have to poop inside, but they still can't go in the pasture. They're not getting the exercise they should, either. Your dad and grandmother wash the runs out two times a day, but it all flows out the end of the barn. Once we get the dogs back on their regular schedule, it won't be so bad."

"Promise?"

"Well . . . not *quite* as bad."

The roar of a jet engine made my muscles

tighten. As it drew closer, the noise—a deafening screaming roar—made my neck kind of scrunch down between my shoulders like a turtle trying to duck inside his shell. The noise grew so loud, the walls of the old barn seemed to shake. I could swear I saw dust falling between the boards.

"Watch the hose, Tom. Try not to get it wet inside the doghouses."

When I glanced down, the water spray was landing two pens away. A little Brittany spaniel flopped her ears, shook, and darted into the safety of her doghouse.

"Sorry."

The rumbling from above finally faded. I concentrated on spraying the doggy poop out of the pens. Most of it rolled. Tumbling with the spray and force of the water, it finally fell over the edge and into the trough. The wet stuff . . . well, it just kind of broke apart. Sometimes it stuck on the chain-link and I had to keep the hose on it a little longer.

I'd only gotten to three more pens when another jet took off. My neck scrunched down between my shoulders and my eyes clamped shut. But only for a second. I didn't want to soak another poor dog, so I forced them to open.

My grandfather's dog kennel was really an old dairy barn. The farm was here long before they built the airport. When the farmer who used to own the place retired, Grandpa bought it. Even though it was real close to the airport, he thought it would be a good place to raise and train his bird dogs. Besides, Grandpa had told me that, after a while, he got used to the noise. I didn't see how that could ever happen.

Then about a year after they came to live here, the airport needed to expand. They built a new runway west of the others. That put the flight path right over their house. It made for a lot of noise, but Grandma and Grandpa didn't mind. The dogs didn't seem bothered by it either.

Grandpa used the old hay barn for storage, a place to keep a couple of horses, and a pigeon coop with about ten birds. He also put part of the dog pens on the south side—protected from the north wind in the winter, and shaded by the long, sloping, roof overhang in the summer. Grandma turned the two brooding houses (where the farmer's wife raised baby chickens) into places for the mother dogs to have their puppies.

The dairy barn worked perfect for the main kennel. Made of concrete, the whole floor sloped a little to the east. It was so slight I couldn't even notice it. And about where the cows' tails would be, when they were being milked, there was a trough in the concrete, on both sides of the barn. Grandpa said that when the farmer poured the floor, he probably just laid down a couple of twelve-inch boards. When the concrete dried, he pulled them up and had his trough. That way he could wash out whatever mess the cows made, and not have to clean the entire barn until he was through milking.

Grandpa built six dog pens on each side of the barn. Each had a doggy door so the dogs could get outside to a concrete run he had built. That still left a wide empty space, in the middle of the barn. So Grandpa built six more pens there.

Those were the ones Mama and I saved for last, because they were the most important to keep clean.

"Want to spray down those last three pens?"

Mama's voice jerked me from my memories. My head snapped up.

"What?"

"Spray down those last three pens," she repeated, more like an order this time instead of a question. "That trough's about as clean as it's going to get. All you're doing is running water."

I glanced down. Sure enough, there wasn't anything left. Just three more pens, then we could go see Grandma and Grandpa—and go home. Trouble was, there were still dogs in the last two.

"Aren't you going to let those two out? Aren't we supposed to let them run for a few minutes?"

"No!"

The way Mama snapped at me made me jerk my hand. I accidentally sprayed the dog in the next to the last pen.

"No," she repeated, softer this time. "Your grandmother said that the female is young and really high-strung. She's not trained to come, so we'd need to put a leash on her. She's also a fraidy-cat. Your grandmother's afraid she might bite someone she doesn't know.

"The other one is Old Gabe. We don't let him out at all."

"That's not fair," I protested.

Mama nodded. "You're right. It's not fair. But only your grandfather can let him out."

"Why?"

"He's Old Gabe." Mama shrugged.

I finished spraying the last pen. The dog there didn't bark or spin around like some of the others had. He just lay in his doghouse and watched me. When I was done, I turned to wash the waste out of the trough.

"Why can't we let him out?" I asked again, looking at Mama instead of him.

A roaring, snapping, slashing growl sent the hair standing straight up on the back of my neck. The chain-link fence rattled. I could swear I heard the gate fly open.

Without even glancing back, I dropped the water hose and took off.

43

When I finally realized nothing was snapping at my heels, I stopped and turned.

The dog in the last pen stood with his front paws against the fence. Still growling and snarling, he shook the wire and glared at me. I glared back—mad that he'd scared me.

Then I could almost see a grin on his face.

He wagged his tail and trotted back to lie down in his doghouse, just as cool and calm as if he'd intended to make me jump clean out of my socks.

Only after he disappeared inside did I realize how far I'd run. I'd stopped a good ten feet outside the doorway. Right where all the water, and mud, and doggy-doo flowed out and into the pasture.

When I looked down, I felt my nose crinkle and my toes curl. The mud and goo was oozing—clear up over the top of my tennis shoes.

"That's why," Mama called.

Chapter 7

Grandma met us at the back door. She glanced down at my muddy shoes, and sighed.

"You been playing in the mud? Or did you meet Old Gabe?"

Mama giggled. When I glared at her, she clamped a hand over her mouth—only I could still see her eyes twinkling. She helped me hose down my tennis shoes. Then I pulled off my socks, and she ran the water over my feet. Grandma got me a pair of Grandpa's old coaching shorts from his drawer, and she put my tennis shoes, socks, and jeans in the washer. My pants weren't really that muddy, but what with tearing through the slop, I did get splatters on them.

Grandpa's shorts were a little big, so I had

to hold them with one hand when I followed Grandma and Mama to the bedroom.

Grandpa sat on the edge of the bed, clutching a pillow against his chest.

"You're not supposed to get up without someone in here to help," Grandma scolded.

"I'm not *getting* up, I'm just *sitting* up."

When he saw us in the doorway, Grandpa smiled. Instantly the smile disappeared. He took a deep breath and coughed, his face wrinkled to a grimace, teeth gritted, eyes clinched shut, and tendons in his neck bulging out with the strain.

"Oh . . . man, that hurts." He sighed, loosening his grip on the pillow. "Them doctors split me open like a ripe melon." The grimace returned to his face—like he was bracing himself—then he coughed again. Little beads of sweat popped out on his forehead. Grandpa sat for a moment, breathing soft and easy, until he caught his breath.

"Sorry about that. Doctors told me to cough a lot. Keeps the fluid from collecting in my lungs, so I don't get pneumonia. Sure do hurt, though."

He slipped a hand between himself and the pillow and patted his chest, very gently.

46

"How you doing, Tom? Glad school's out for the summer?"

"Yes, sir." I smiled. "I sure am."

Holding his breath a moment, as if fighting back another cough, he nodded at Mama.

"How about you, Jillian? Any problems at work? Your boss give you any static about leaving the office early?"

Mama leaned forward and kissed him on the cheek.

"No. I offered to come in at seven, so I could make up the time I missed. That way Tom and I could get here around four or so to help Mama. Johnny said not to worry about it. Said family's more important, and that's what I needed to be taking care of right now."

"How about the dogs? Any problems out there?"

Mama shook her head. "Everything went just fine." She paused a moment, her eyes cut toward me. "Well . . ."

I felt my mouth twist up on one side when I saw the twinkle in her eye.

"Old Gabe pulled a sneak attack on Tom."

47

Grandpa shot her a stern look. "You didn't let him out, did you?"

"No. He was still in his pen, but . . ."

"Jumped on the fence and started snarling and barking, right?"

Mama smiled at Grandpa. "Right."

Grandpa only got in one little laugh before his eyes flashed. He clutched the pillow and started coughing again.

Grandma motioned us toward the door. "Got cheese and turkey in the fridge. You and Tom go fix yourselves a sandwich. I'll wait till he's through coughing, and tuck him back in bed. Oh, there's chips in the pantry."

Mama and I went to the kitchen.

"Is Grandpa gonna be okay?" I asked.

"Huh?"

Mama didn't hear me because she had her head in the fridge.

"Is Grandpa gonna be okay?" I repeated. "I mean, with all that coughing and stuff?"

"White or wheat?"

"White."

"Your grandpa's fine, Tom. Triple bypass surgery used to be very dangerous. Nowadays, it's pretty simple. He has to take it easy for a while, though."

"But the way he grabs his chest . . . I mean, his face and . . . and, well . . . it really looks like it hurts."

"I imagine it *does* hurt," she said. "The doctors explained that his heart is working fine now. The pain comes from the muscles in his chest and his ribs trying to mend. It's normal."

Grandma came in, opened the pantry door, and stretched up on her tiptoes. "Barbecue or plain?"

"Plain," Mama answered.

"And barbecue," I added.

She brought both packages of chips and laid them on the bar. They started talking about Grandpa, and the dogs, and a bunch of other stuff while they were making the sandwiches.

After supper, Grandma went with us to feed.

"It's right simple, once you get the hang of it," she explained as we followed her to the big barn.

Just inside the door, on the right, was a box made of concrete blocks. It had a sheet of iron for a top. Grandma twisted the latch and lifted it. It must have been heavier than it looked, judging by the way her muscles strained.

"Don't get your hand in the way when you close the lid," she warned. "Thing's heavy enough to take a finger or two clean off."

Inside the box were a bunch of dog food sacks, all standing on end in neat rows.

"The ones on the left are for the mama dogs. They're higher in protein and have some added nutrients that they need when they're nursing their pups." She picked up a coffee can. "Angie's got a litter of seven. Since she's nursing, I usually give her about a can and a half." She dumped the dog food into a plastic bucket, then dipped the coffee can into the dog food sack again. "Sal is expecting any day now. Till the pups get here, I keep her at one pound." Dumping that into the bucket, she glanced over her shoulder and winked at Mama. "Don't want her to lose her girlish figure."

Next she leaned over and lifted a sack from the rows on the right. She took hold of the little string that stuck out from one corner, and ripped the sack open. She poured that into the plastic bucket.

"Been doing this ever since your grandpa had his heart attack. Gettin' used to it."

Once the first plastic bucket was full, she poured more food in a second bucket.

"This is the regular dog food. Everybody gets a one-pound coffee can." Her eyes cut to the side as she glanced first one way, then the other. "All right, not everybody. There are two Brittany females—one in the center run where Old Gabe is, the other on the south side of this barn. They're kind of small, so I usually just give them three-quarters of a can. Ty is the biggest darned bird dog I ever saw in my life. Sweet as he can be. Just big." She pointed to the south side of the hay barn. "Your grandpa's not training him, he's just boarding him for a fella down in Dallas. That dog can scarf down two cans without batting an eye. Old Gabe gets a little more, too. But I'll feed him myself. Neither one of you need to mess with him."

"I can't believe he's still so mean and nasty," Mama said. "I figured, when he got up in years, he'd kind of mellow out."

Grandma gave a little laugh. "Old rascal's just like your dad, Jillian. He ain't never gonna mellow out."

It was dark by the time Mama and I got home. The last day of school I usually played with Danny and Mark. We threw a baseball, or played setback with the football, or just horsed around.

But it had been a long day. I mean—*really long*!

I gave Daddy a hug, tossed my backpack in the closet, took a shower, and climbed into bed.

I was asleep before the sheet even settled!

 Chapter 8

Daddy didn't have to work on the weekend, so all three of us went to help with the dogs. We also visited with Grandpa, but mostly he slept. Mama and Grandma fixed baked beans and scalloped potatoes. Daddy and I cooked hamburgers on Grandpa's grill.

After dinner Mama and Grandma drove to an office supply store. I don't know what the thing was called, but they brought back this little hand-held machine that you could make plastic labels with. The strips were about a half-inch wide, and the back peeled off so we could stick them to the gate on the dog pens.

Some dog trainers teach their dogs to come by

whistling. Others use a police whistle. Grandpa trains his dogs to come when he calls their name.

Only trouble, Mama and I didn't know their names.

Things had been so hectic since Grandpa got sick that the dogs had hardly had a good run. They really needed some exercise.

Grandma and Mama were cleaning the pens on the south side of the big barn while Daddy and I handled the others. Each time Grandma finished, she'd let a dog run. While the dog was flying around the barn and across the pasture, she'd make a name tag and stick it to the pole beside its gate.

It took a while. Between squeezing the machine so the letters came through on the plastic strip, and having to trot back to the house to ask Grandpa when she forgot a dog's name, Daddy and I were already finished with our side.

So we helped with the name-making thingy. It really was hard to get those letters to come through. I mean, you had to squeeze like mad. I only did about five names before my hand and fingers got numb. Daddy took it for a while.

Tess was the name of the high-strung little pointer bird dog in the pen next to Gabe. I made her name tag. Grandma had me put the word "wild" in parentheses next to it. She was the one who didn't mind very well and didn't come when called. I stood way back from Old Gabe's pen when I made his name. (Not that I really needed to make a nameplate for him.) After scaring me into the doggy poop yesterday, I knew good and well I'd never forget him. As I squeezed the letters onto the plastic strip, I watched him out of the corner of my eye. Any second I expected him to come barking, and roaring, and slamming against the fence. He didn't. He just lay in his doghouse and watched *me* out of the corner of *his* eye.

I held my breath when I stuck the name tag to his gatepost. He still didn't move. *Bet he's waiting till I turn my back on him,* I thought. *That's when he'll launch his sneak attack.*

Still holding the air inside my lungs, I turned my back and braced. When nothing happened, I moved away, still stiff. *Stay ready. Any second now.*

.   .   .

A whole week went by and Old Gabe never tried to scare me. I was ready for him, but he never once jumped at the fence like he was gonna tear me up.

That first week, I got to sleep late. I was awake enough to hear when Mama and Daddy left for work, but I stayed in bed. Around ten or so I'd get up and fix something for breakfast.

The second week, Little League baseball started. So did a three-week soccer camp. Mr. Storms, our soccer coach, called and said they had two young men from England coming this year. He said they were really good.

It was a hard decision to make. Danny and Mark wanted me to play baseball this summer and I wanted to be with my friends. But I liked soccer a whole lot more than baseball.

Soccer camp lasted from seven-thirty until one, and I sure hated getting up that early. Mama would drop me off on her way to work and Daddy would pick me up on his lunch hour and run me back home. When Mama got home, she and I drove out to the kennel, cleaned dog pens, fed dogs, and visited. Then it was back home, eat supper, and go to sleep so I could get up in time for soccer.

Grandma didn't let Grandpa out of the house until near the end of the second week. Then she only let him as far as the porch.

Whenever we let a dog loose to exercise, Grandpa clutched a pillow over his chest. Every one of those dogs was so glad to see him, they'd race straight for him. Some cowed down, all bashful and shylike. Wiggling and easing close, they'd wait until he leaned over to pet them, then go tearing off. Others would try to jump up so he'd pet them.

That's what the pillow was for.

Grandpa used it kind of like a shield to keep the dogs from jabbing him in the chest with their paws.

Friday of the third week, Grandma let him wander out into the yard. He petted the dogs when they came to greet him, but mostly Grandma wanted him to walk. "Doctor said he needs to start exercising," she told us.

I was almost through feeding my dogs when Grandpa waved me over. "There are some wooden pegs next to the feed box, in the big barn," he said.

"Get that thick cotton rope with a leather collar clipped to it. Tess really needs to run. Make sure the collar's tight. Don't choke her, but get it tight enough so she can't slip it over her head." He turned and started back for the porch. "I'm gonna go get my pillow and sit down. Crazy as that little pup is, she'd probably wrap the rope around my legs and end up dumping me on my nose. Hang on to the rope until I call her. Need to work on getting her to respond to her name."

Grandpa hobbled along. I found the long rope with the collar and was almost back to Tess's pen before he went inside. Keeping my foot and knee in the opening, so she couldn't slip past, I squeezed inside and put the collar on her.

It wasn't easy, what with her wiggling and trying to jump up on me. Once I had it around her neck, I slipped my finger under it. I tightened it another notch and turned to open the gate. Leaning against the chain-link, I reached for the latch.

The snarling, roaring growl sent the hairs at the back of my neck bristling. Goose bumps popped up on my arms and across my shoulders. Something hit the fence where I leaned. I could swear I felt teeth sink into my flesh.

I jumped and tripped over Tess. She yelped.

I remember falling. I remember trying to grab the gate and catch myself. But I didn't remember anything else until I landed on the far side of the pen, with my left ear, cheek, and head in her water bowl.

Sitting up, I wiped the water off my face and out of my eyes. I could have sworn Old Gabe bit me through the fence, but there wasn't a mark on me.

Old Gabe sat in front of his doghouse. Wagging his tail and watching me, I could swear the old dog was smiling from ear to floppy ear.

I crawled to my feet, stomped over, and kicked the chain-link.

Now come and get me! I raged inside my head. *Come bite at the fence again. I'll kick you right in the nose.*

Old Gabe just sat there, smiling.

Something brushed against my ankle. I jerked my foot away from whatever touched me, and glanced down.

The tail end of a cotton rope whipped around the gate. Spinning and flopping, it slid down the concrete floor and disappeared around the corner of the barn.

"Tess," I breathed.

She was gone.

What if Grandpa wasn't sitting down? What if he didn't have his pillow against his chest and she jumped on him?

"Tess!"

I screamed the name this time. I raced out of the pen, running as hard as I could.

Chapter 9

When I rounded the far corner of the barn, my eyes sprang wide open. Grandpa was just coming through the front door. Holding his pillow down at his side, he turned to make sure the screen was shut. He wasn't paying a bit of attention.

"Tess!" I screamed.

If nothing else, maybe he'd hear me and be ready if she jumped on him.

"Tess?" I called the name again. Only this time it wasn't a scream. It was more like a question. Tess wasn't headed for Grandpa, like all the other dogs had done.

Tess was no place in sight.

I glanced left. Right. Behind me. She wasn't there.

Grandpa must have heard me yelling for her. When I looked back at him, he waved his pillow at the big barn.

"She inside with the other dogs?" I asked as I ran past him.

"Far side. Headed out to the horse pasture."

The dogs in the big barn barked when I raced past. At the far side of the barn, there was still no sign of Tess. I climbed up on the big metal gate.

Joe and Ginger were munching grass in the middle of the field. Swishing flies with their tails, their heads suddenly sprang up, their ears perked straight for the sky, and they stampeded across the pasture, racing toward the gate.

That's when I finally spotted Tess.

Grandpa's horses weren't afraid of dogs—they were used to them. But the big cotton rope flopping through the grass behind Tess must have spooked them.

I spotted that rope before I saw her. She was running so hard and fast, the tail end of the rope was flipping and bouncing clear above the tall grass. Floppy ears waving in the wind, Tess was at the other end of it.

Soccer is a pretty good sport. Nathan and Jerome, the guys who were doing our three-week soccer camp, worked with us on ball-handling skills. We'd practice trapping the ball, heading, and using our bodies to bring down a pass. We had to bounce the ball twenty times with our right foot and twenty times with our left without letting it touch the ground. And we practiced dribbling. We'd also sprint from one end of the field and back—running as hard as we could, but still keeping control of the ball. We dribbled around cones— changing pace, sprinting, trapping the ball to a dead stop, dribbling—slow and changing direction, fast and changing direction. Then we ran some more.

Not only is soccer a good sport, it comes in handy sometimes.

If I hadn't spent two weeks doing all that running at soccer camp, I would have probably never caught Tess.

That stupid dog ran me all over the horse pasture. She slipped under the fence and made it halfway across the airport property before she circled back. I finally trapped the rope with my foot, like I trapped a soccer ball. Only the bird dog was running so fast, she just ripped it from under me.

The next time I caught up with the end of that rope, I pounced on it with both feet.

Forget soccer, I'm so out of breath I'm about to drop.

Tess hit the end of the rope at full speed. She flipped herself over backwards, got up, shook herself, and tried to take off again. I had her this time, though.

Looping the rope around my arm and hand like an electrical cord, I pulled her to me. Rope and dog in tow, I dragged her back to the kennels and to Grandpa.

Both of us were still panting by the time we got to the porch. That didn't keep Tess from lunging and pulling at the rope. Her tongue was almost dragging on the ground when I sat on the steps.

"What happened?" Grandpa sighed.

"That darned Gabe," I gasped. "I was watching Tess really close. You know—being careful not to let her out till I had a good hold on the rope. He jumped up and tried to bite my arm through the chain-link." I stopped, sucking in more oxygen.

"Why do you keep that darned old dog anyway, Grandpa?"

He pulled a cigar from the table beside his chair and started chewing on it. He didn't light it, though. Between the heart attack, the surgery, the doctor, and Grandma fussing at him, he finally figured out that smoking wasn't that good an idea.

"Gabe's my honors dog," Grandpa answered.

"Huh?"

"Honors dog. He helps me train the pups to honor point."

I shook my head. "I don't understand, Grandpa. What's an honors dog? What's honor point?"

Grandpa took the cigar out of his mouth, used his tongue to pick a little piece of tobacco from between his teeth, and spit.

"Okay. You've seen a dog point, right?"

I nodded, remembering how they freeze, tail all straight and stiff, and usually a front paw tucked up by their chest.

"If you're hunting with more than one dog, they'll both point singles—one dog will come down on point, another dog will stumble on a different bird and lock up. But when they're working a covey, usually one dog will spot them before the others. Honor means that the dogs point the first dog. They trust his judgment—that he's found birds—and stop, dead in their tracks, to point the dog, instead of trying to find the birds themselves."

My brow wrinkled.

"It's a hard thing for even the smartest bird dog pup to learn. They're *bred* to hunt birds. They want to keep running until they find the covey. End up tearing through the birds and flushing them." He spit another piece of tobacco. Nodded toward the rope wrapped in my hand. "Even tugging on the rope and yelling at them can't make them understand, sometimes.

"But Old Gabe's got a way of communicating with them. It ain't too pretty. But that old dog's taught a hundred and fifty, maybe two hundred pups, about honor."

I guess the look on my face was enough for Grandpa.

"Doctor said I could get back to work next week." He smiled. "I'll take you out with one of the pups who's almost finished, and show you."

"He said you could work, but *just a little*."

Grandpa and I both jumped. We hadn't seen or heard Grandma come to the screen door. "He also said you weren't to lift anything heavier than a newspaper, remember? That included yanking on a rope with some wild pup pulling on the other end."

Grandpa stuck the cigar back in his mouth. Raised an eyebrow at her.

"You sure?"

"I asked him about that, specifically." Grandma smiled. "Those were his exact words."

Grandpa folded his arms and glared at her. "Well, I won't pull hard. I'll just work with the more experienced dogs and—"

"And," Grandma butted in, "you'll end up busting your incision open and we'll have to rush you back to the hospital—*if* we're lucky."

"Now, Beth," he soothed. "Don't get all worked up."

"I'm not gettin' all worked up. I'm just stating

facts, you old coot. You gotta take care of yourself or—"

"Hey, I got an idea." I don't know whether I really had a good idea, or if I was just trying to keep them from arguing. "Soccer camp is over on Saturday. Indoor soccer doesn't start until September. I could help Grandpa train the pups."

When they both stopped to stare at me, I shrugged.

"Well, there's nothing else to do. I could sit home and watch TV. But after ten, there's nothing on but soap operas and talk shows. Maybe Mama or Daddy could bring me out on their way to work. Or . . . or maybe I could spend a night or two . . . or something."

Grandpa picked a piece of tobacco off his tongue, rolled it between his finger and thumb, then flipped it on the ground.

"I guess I could tell Tom what needs to be done. How to do it. Just might work."

I shrugged again.

"Yeah, Grandma. It might be fun."

Chapter 10

Soccer camp was fun.

Nathan and Jerome were both really good. They showed us a lot of things. It was neat to listen to them talk, too. Their English accents made them a little hard to understand sometimes. Whether they were around or not, almost all of us tried to imitate them. They got as tickled as we did.

Short and kind of stocky, Nathan had muscles like you wouldn't believe. But Jerome was my favorite—especially his legs. Jerome was tall and skinny. I'd never seen legs as long as his. When I first saw him run, he looked kind of clumsy and disconnected. But he could do *unbelievable* things with a soccer ball.

He could sprint down the field, as fast as the

wind, jump and land on the ball—with both feet at the same time, no less. Then spin in midair and race off to the side before we could even get stopped. He was always laughing and telling us jokes, too.

Jerome always waited on his jokes until the girls were off working with Nathan. That's probably because a lot of them were kind of dirty. Some, I didn't even get. But both the guys were fun to be around and fun to listen to.

Six Flags was fun, too.

Mama talked to Grandma on Thursday. She thought Grandpa needed a couple more days before he started working again. She told Mama that if they didn't start bringing me out to help him until Tuesday or Wednesday, it would make it easier on her to keep him inside.

Daddy said we didn't have much money or time for a vacation this year, but driving down to Six Flags would give us a little break. All three of us talked it over and decided we'd go down Saturday night, spend Sunday and Monday at the park, then just lie around the house on Tuesday.

Saturday, after soccer camp, we loaded in the car and headed out. We didn't even try to go to the park on Saturday evening, since it was always too crowded on Saturdays. So we kind of hung around the motel. All three of us swam and played in the pool. I found some guys about my own age to swim and play with, while Mama and Daddy visited and made friends with the grown-ups.

It was late when we got to bed. But it was still hard to get to sleep. It'd been two years since we'd come to the amusement park, and I guess I was excited about checking out some of the new rides. I spent a lot of time flipping and flopping, until I finally settled down and dozed off.

Superman and the Thunderbolt were my two favorites. I take that back. I always loved the log ride and the Roaring Rapids. But of the new rides, the Thunderbolt and Superman were the best!

There was a long line at Superman. Daddy didn't like heights, so he chickened out. Said he'd wait for us. When we finally got to the front of the line, the attendant opened the gate, told us not to run, and stepped aside. Everybody ran.

Nobody ran when we got off.

Mama said it was exciting, but if I wanted to go again she'd wait with Daddy.

A teenage boy—I guess he was about fifteen or sixteen—had to sit next to me, because each bench held three people. The guy acted real cool and calm, but he never said a word.

He screamed a lot, though. I never knew guys could scream that loud and shrill. He was about six feet behind us when we came out the exit gate. Yelling and shouting, a bunch of his friends came rushing up. They surrounded him asking all sorts of questions—"Was it scary? Was it fun? Did you like it?"

He just laughed and told them it was kind of a sissy ride, and he wanted to go on something more exciting.

It was all I could do to keep from turning around and laughing out loud.

The Thunderbolt was a big, wooden roller coaster. The attendant stuck me about three seats behind Mama and Daddy, with a girl about my age. She was kinda cute. She smiled when I sat down, but neither one of us said anything.

The cars clunked and rattled as we chugged to the top. I could swear the first hill was higher than Superman—and that was the tallest ride I'd ever been on.

Then we slowly went over the top.

It was wild! Steep and fast, some of the curves made me feel like I was going to fly out. The way the cars rattled and clunked, I could picture the whole thing jumping off the tracks, and sailing out across the park on the very next turn.

It scared me, but I didn't scream like the teenage boy did. I *did* know that we'd probably never get Daddy on it again.

That's why it surprised me when he and Mama were waiting at the end of the exit ramp. They grabbed my hands and practically dragged me back to the entrance.

The third time they wanted to ride, I told them I needed to go to the bathroom. I'd wait for them at the bench by the ice cream parlor. They rode the thing three more times before they were ready to race on to something else. I was kind of glad they did. It gave my stomach time to settle down.

That night, at the pool, Mama and Daddy went

to the hot tub. The girl who rode the Thunderbolt with me was there with her parents. I went to play in the pool while they visited.

Monday was fantastic!

There was hardly anybody in the park. We could run from one ride to the next. Go straight to the front, and practically hop on without having to wait.

About noon Mama and Daddy pooped out.

We found a place to grab a hamburger, fries, and a fountain drink, then went outside to the seating area.

"John. Jillian," someone called. "Over here."

It was the people from last night, the ones with the girl. I followed Mama and Daddy to the table. Before I even got my leg over the bench, Daddy motioned to me with his tray.

"This is our son, Thomas. Thomas, this is Daniel, Margie, and Angie Sullivan. They're from Minnesota. Angie's going to be in sixth grade next year, too."

I smiled.

"Well," Mama urged. "Say hello."

I smiled again. "Hi."

The girl smiled back, nodded, then stuck another french fry in her mouth. Her mom and dad said hello, then started visiting with Mama and Daddy, again. Every once in a while they'd ask me something like what sports I liked, what sort of things my friends and I did after school. Mama and Daddy asked the girl what her favorite subject was and stuff like that. I guess our parents were just being polite and trying to include both of us in their conversation. But I don't think either one of us was that interested. I didn't know about her, but I just wanted to finish eating so I could hit the rides again.

Besides that, I didn't like sitting across from a girl. Not while I was trying to eat, anyway. I don't know *why* I didn't like it. I just didn't.

While our parents chatted, Angie and I just sat and tried not to look at each other. Finally Mama leaned toward me.

"I don't think Angie is going to bite you," she teased.

"Huh?"

"You and Angie can visit," she encouraged. "I met her last night. She's really nice."

I smiled at Mama. Smiled at Angie. And took another bite of my hamburger.

Mama's look was a bit more stern when she leaned over a few minutes later. "Say something to her, Tom," she whispered. "Angie doesn't have anybody to visit with. No sense in you just sitting there like a lump on a log."

I swallowed the bite of hamburger—hoping it would help me swallow the lump in my throat when it went down. I didn't know what to say. So I went with the first thing that popped into my head.

"My grandpa has a dog named Angie. She's got puppies."

 Chapter 11

It took me more than an hour to work up the nerve.

"Okay," I asked finally, right before our raft went under the waterfall, "what was that look about?"

"What look?" Angie's smile was sweet and innocent as could be. "I don't have the slightest idea what you're talking about."

The raft swung around just as we went under the falls. A bunch of high school girls on the opposite side squealed and laughed. Then they batted the water with their hands, trying to get the rest of us as wet as they were.

Our parents had dragged us around on about five or six different rides. I don't know whether it had been on purpose or not, but they kept getting on things that seated two people—together—instead of three or four. That left me stuck with Angie. Then they'd found a place to sit in the shade, and "suggested" that we go ahead and hit the rides while they rested.

After the Roaring Rapids, we went to the swinging ship, then to the log ride. There was absolutely no one in line there. So they stuck us in a log all by ourselves, waited a moment, and when no one else came running down the ramp, they launched us on our way. I sat way in the front. Angie sat way in the back.

After the first drop—when we started floating gently down the trough—I swung my leg over the bench and turned around to face her.

"Look. If I said something wrong—I'm sorry. At least let me know *what* I said."

"You just don't know how to talk to a girl, do you?" She tossed her head to get the long strands of blonde hair out of her eyes.

Straddling the bench, facing her, all I could do was hold out my hands, helplessly, and shrug.

"You're right. I don't. Fact is, I usually try *not* to talk to girls, unless I absolutely have to. Now what did I say that made you so mad?"

She sighed and rolled her eyes.

"Please?"

"Okay. When someone introduces you, you should say something nice—like, 'Hello. It's a pleasure to meet you.' Or you could say, 'Angie. What a lovely name.' You don't just blurt out, 'Duh . . . I got me a dog,'" she drawled, trying to imitate my southern accent. "Her name's the same as yours. She done went and had puppies."

I felt my lip curl.

"That's not what I said. And I don't talk like that. People from Minnesota are the ones who talk funny. And . . . and, well . . . Angie belongs to my grandpa. He raises and trains bird dogs. She's nice, and . . . well . . . okay, I apologize for not saying something polite."

She just sat and stared at me.

I guess I could have done a better job of sounding sincere. I cleared my throat. "I'm sorry. Really. Okay?"

Angie's lips curled toward a smile. But the

corners only got about halfway up when her eyes suddenly flashed wide, and her mouth fell open.

I didn't even have time to glance over my shoulder when something jerked the log and lurched me forward. The cogs beneath us caught on the rail. A quick glance told me we were on the last steep climb before we plunged into the water at the end of the ride.

I let go with one hand and tried to swing my leg over. But the slope was so steep that as soon as I let go, I slid. Now I was in the middle of the log.

Maybe I can get my leg over, then turn—real quick, catch myself, and . . .

That didn't work, either. As soon as I lifted my foot, the other foot slipped on the wet floor.

Pushing with both legs, and holding as tight as I could with both hands, didn't help, either. By the time we neared the top, I'd slid all the way to the back of the car. Our knees were crammed together, and Angie's eyes were so big around, I thought they might pop clean out of her head.

"Hang on," I yelled. "As soon as we start over, I'll spin and try to brace us. Hold on."

We slowed at the peak. I yanked my leg from the floor and spun on my bottom.

I got turned, only . . .

We were going down.

No. We weren't going down—we were *flying* down. Wind pushed the breath back into my throat. It whipped a strand of long blonde hair across my eyes.

I grabbed for the side of the log, but I couldn't get a good grip. My feet weren't planted, either. The harder I shoved on the floor of the log, the more my tennis shoes slipped and slid.

We were almost at the bottom. In a second or two, the front of the log would hit the water and . . .

THIS IS GONNA HURT!

I leaned back. Lifted both feet. Aimed them at the front of the log. Arms bent, just a little, my muscles tensed to help catch us if my legs didn't hold. My teeth clinched tight. I could hear them grinding inside my skull, and . . .

And . . .

The next thing I knew, we were both totally

drenched. Angie's cheek was tight against my left ear. I could hear her laughing. I could hear me laughing.

One of Angie's arms was wrapped around my head, the other around my chest. She was plastered against my back like wallpaper, and the padded bar at the front of the log was shoved so far into my stomach, I could hardly breathe— much less laugh.

But that's exactly what we were doing. Both of us were laughing our fool heads off.

Angie scooted back by the time we got to the attendant. It felt good to get the padded bar out of my stomach, and my thumb knuckles out from under my ribs. The attendant held the log against the side with her foot and reached out a hand to help me. I turned to help Angie, who looked like a drowned rat. Long blonde hair plastered against her face. Water dripping from her shorts plopped in little puddles beside her feet. I guess I was just as wet. When she looked at me, she giggled.

"Let's do it again." Both of us laughed at the exact same moment. Water squishing and sloshing inside our tennis shoes, we sprinted up the ramp and back around to the entrance.

We talked and laughed and . . . I didn't even realize we were still holding hands until we had to let go to get into the log.

"You have fun today?" Mama asked when I finished brushing my teeth and climbed into the roll-away bed next to theirs.

I nodded.

"That Angie's a cute little thing." Daddy raised up from his pillow to peek over the top of his magazine. "Was she fun? Did you like her?"

Angie's GREAT!

That's what I wanted to say. I wanted to tell Mama and Daddy that this was the best trip *ever* to Six Flags. I wanted to tell them that Angie wasn't like the girls at school. She didn't act snooty. She was just fun.

I wanted to tell them that we could talk or hold hands or laugh at dumb stuff. I didn't have to act mean or tough when I was around her. None of the guys were watching. I didn't have to worry about them saying stuff like "Tom's got a girlfriend," or singing "Tom and Angie, sittin' in a tree . . ."

I wanted to tell them that I didn't have to impress her or act cool. We'd never see each other again. They had to go back to Minnesota and we had to get back to help Grandpa with the dogs. So . . . we could both just be ourselves and have fun.

I wanted to tell them that, and a whole lot more about the way I felt, and . . . and . . .

"She's okay—for a girl."

That's all I said.

Despite the sly smile that curled his lip, Daddy just lay back on the pillow and held the magazine in front of his face.

"Well, if she's okay . . ." He paused to turn the page. "I guess you wouldn't mind if we stayed an extra day, and went to Water World with the Sullivans tomorrow."

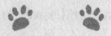 Chapter 12

Soccer camp was fun.

Six Flags was fun.

Water World was . . . it was . . .

Well, there simply weren't words to describe it.

The Sullivans checked out of the motel the same time we did and followed us to Water World. Parked right next to us.

We swam and played and dunked each other. We talked about friends and school and Grandpa's puppies. We talked about fun stuff and even serious stuff. We ran to every single ride in the whole park—then laughed and talked some more.

It was almost dark when Mama and Daddy said it was time to start home.

Mr. Sullivan, Daddy, and I changed out of our wet clothes in the bathhouse. We waited for Angie and the moms, then headed for the cars. While the grown-ups were saying their good-byes, I went to stick my bathing suit and towel in the trunk.

I reached up to close the lid, but my fingers slipped off when I tried to pull it down. It was like the thing was stuck or something. I glanced up. Angie stood behind me, holding the trunk lid. She put her free hand on my shoulder and turned me so I was facing her. Then she let go of the trunk and put that arm around my neck and . . .

She kissed me—right on the mouth.

Vicky Fargus tried to kiss me one time, on the playground. I'd shoved her away, shook my fist in her face, and told her if she ever did that again, I'd bust her right in the nose.

Now I just stood there. Darned if Angie didn't kiss me again.

She stuffed a little piece of paper into my hand. "I know we'll probably never see each other again. You can e-mail me, if you want to. But you don't have to."

I looked at the little piece of crinkled-up paper, nodded, and smiled at her. "I will."

She arched an eyebrow.

"I will. Promise."

"Thank you," she said. "You made this the most wonderful vacation I ever had."

When she smiled, her eyes sparkled like stars flickering in a cloudless night sky.

I could still see them when I looked up at the clear . . .

"Tom?"

"Yes, dear," I breathed.

"Thomas!"

The sound of Grandpa's gruff voice made me jerk. I blinked a couple of times. I wasn't looking up at the stars twinkling in the clear night sky. I was staring up at the roof of the barn. Grandpa stood beside me, his head tilted far to the side, his eyes opened so wide, it almost made him look like he had hair on the front of his bald head again.

"What, Grandpa?"

"Got the lead rope wrapped around my legs." He pointed. "And you're choking the dog."

"Sorry." I unwrapped the rope, then knelt and rubbed the dog's throat until he stopped coughing. "I was thinking about something else."

"It's like you're a hundred miles off. Been that way all morning. Now pay attention to what we're doing, so we can work these last two dogs and . . . and . . ." He paused a moment, looking around, then sighed.

"Tell you what, Tom. I got a better idea. Why don't you go help your grandmother with the puppies?"

I puffed my chest out and stood straight. "I'll pay attention, Grandpa. Really. I'm serious."

"I'm serious, too." His smile was gentle—not mean or irritated. "This dog doesn't fight the rope, so I won't have to pull or strain. Besides that, I'm starving. If you go move Angie's pups for Grandma, she can start dinner. Then we can eat."

Frowning, I studied him for a moment. Sure he was being honest with me, I smiled back at him. "Yes, sir."

I'd only taken a step or two when I heard a

weird snort. Glancing over my shoulder, I caught Grandpa clamping his lips shut so tight that even his nose was turning white.

"You okay, Grandpa?"

He snorted again and kind of waved a hand, as if shooing me away.

"Just glad you said 'Yes, sir' instead of 'Yes, dear.' Kinda had me worried there for a minute."

I felt the heat rush to my face. My ears burned. They were probably so red, Grandpa could see them glowing. I didn't even turn around. I just took off, like a shot, to go find Grandma.

Grandma was in the old brooding house. The walls were thick, to help keep it cool in the summer. An electric heater was about halfway up the west wall, high enough so neither the mama dog nor the puppies could get too close to it and hurt themselves.

Kind of dark inside, it took a moment for my eyes to adjust to the dim light. Grandma sat on top of a big wooden box filled with old blankets and burlap bags. Holding one of the pups in her lap, she stroked its head and back. Cooing and talking sweet to it, just like it was a real baby. When she noticed me standing there, she ruffled the puppy's head and put it on the floor.

"Grandpa sent me to help move the puppies so you could go start dinner."

She made a grunting sound when she struggled to her feet. "Reckon they are old enough to wean," she said. "But it's always kind of sad when pups have to leave their mama." She knelt and held Angie's face between her hands. "You're a sweet girl," she said, softly. "You've been a good mama. But it's time for them to go." She sighed. "Guess it's just part of growing up," she added—more to herself than to me or Angie.

She picked up two of the pups and nodded toward the others. I got two, then followed her outside.

There was a portable chain-link pen, about thirty yards to the south of the brooding house. Not far from the creek, big trees threw shade across part of the area where it stood. We put our pups down, pushed them back so we could get the gate shut, then went for the last three.

Once all seven of the pups were in the pen, we

went to the barn to get a couple of food bowls and a bucket for water.

"You take the water in and put it on the far side of the pen—there in the shade," she told me. "I'll stay here and try to keep the little rascals from getting out, then hand the feed bowls over the fence to you."

Just getting in the gate was a challenge. The puppies kept jumping at my legs, trying to get me to play with them or let them out so they could run. I figured—real quick—that if I slid my feet instead of walking, it would be easier to get across the pen without stepping on one of them. The bucket was big around, but the sides weren't very tall. That way the puppies could reach over the top to get a drink. What with the wide bucket and the puppies jumping against my legs, I ended up spilling about a third of the water before I could set it in the shade.

Grandma handed the three food bowls over the fence. "Spread them out." She motioned with a wave of her arm. "That way they won't all clump up at one bowl, and they'll each have plenty to eat."

Careful not to step on anybody, I put down the food bowls and made my way back to the gate.

Tumbling over one another, the pups followed me—scampering in front of me, bumping into my feet, and making it next to impossible to walk. It took both Grandma and me to keep them shoved back and get the gate closed.

They stood with their paws on the chain-link, wagging their tails, yapping and bouncing. But for only a moment. Then they took off for the food bowls. Well, not the food *bowls.* Despite having three bowls spread out in the pen, they all managed to clump around one bowl.

Guess I hadn't taken the time to look at them before. In the bright sunlight, with me standing outside the pen where I didn't have to worry about smushing one of them, I finally had the chance.

One pup didn't race to the bowl with the others. He sat at the gate—very straight and proper—and watched us.

"Grandma. Look at this little guy. He's got blue eyes. I never saw a dog with blue eyes before."

When we asked Grandpa, he stopped what he was doing, rushed to put the dog he was working with back in her pen, and took off.

Grandma and I had to trot to keep up with him.

Chapter 13

"Doe-eyed." He smiled.

"Doe-eyed?"

Grandpa nodded. "Yep. Doe-eyed."

Growing up—even before Grandpa had his surgery—we came to visit a lot. And although I wasn't into bird hunting, I knew a little bit about pointers.

There were liver-eared pointers. Those dogs were mostly white with dark brown or liver-colored markings on their ears, sides, and rumps. Angie's litter had a few of those. Then there were lemon-eared pointers. They had pretty much the same markings, only their spots were lighter—sort of a yellow color. Finally were the black-and-whites. They were a fairly new breed. Well, not a new breed—they were still pointers. But their spots were a jet black color, instead of brown or yellow. Three of Angie's pups were black-and-whites.

But all the time I'd been hanging around the kennel and around Grandpa, I'd never heard the term "doe-eyed."

"Doe-eyed?" I wondered out loud.

Grandpa nodded. "When he gets older, the eyes will turn from blue to a light brown color. Kind of like a deer. A doe? You know—doe-eyed."

The other pups were still eating, but the doe-eyed pup sat at the gate watching me. When Grandpa flipped the latch and picked him up, he wiggled, and wagged his tail, and tried to lick Grandpa. But as soon as he closed the gate, the pup spotted me and tried to climb out of Grandpa's arms.

"All the years I've been raising and training pointers, this is only the third one I've seen. The other two were spectacular dogs. Probably the best bird dogs I ever trained. A little neurotic, but still spectacular."

"Neurotic? What's that?"

"Ah—well—," Grandpa stammered. "Different. You know—weird. Nutty. Temperamental.

"Rock was the first. That dog could find birds quicker than any I ever hunted behind. But the old rascal wouldn't retrieve, no matter what.

"He'd pick a bird up and toss it in the air, so I'd know where it was. But I had to go pick the bird up myself, while he went on about his hunting."

"How about the other one?"

Grandpa glanced at me. "Other one?"

"Yeah. You said you only saw two other dogs with blue eyes. What was the other one like?"

"Well, he's not quite as fast to find the birds as Rock was. But in my entire life, I never saw that dog bust a covey."

"What's bust a covey, Grandpa?"

"Flush or scare the birds up, before the hunter gets there. It'll happen to even the best dog. But all the years I hunted with him, not one single time did he scare the birds up before I got there. And that, Tom, is just downright miraculous."

"Did he retrieve? You know, bring the birds back to you?"

"Sure does. Drops 'em right at my feet. Real soft mouth, too. Never chewed a bird."

The pup was leaning so far out of Grandpa's arm, I thought he was going to fall. He stuck out his long pink tongue and licked my arm. I petted him and reached out. He squirmed his way out of Grandpa's arms and into mine.

"You still got him? Is he still around?"

Grandpa nodded and pointed to where Angie stood watching from her pen.

"Yeah. It's Angie's sire. Old Gabe."

I jerked. Without even thinking, I drew my arm away from the pup and his pink tongue, and shoved him back at Grandpa.

"I'm hungry. Let's go eat dinner."

It wasn't that I didn't like puppies. I think every boy does—at least all the guys I knew. And it wasn't that I didn't like that one particular pup. He was kind of special. He caught my attention right off.

Thing was . . . what if he grew up to be like his grandfather—like Old Gabe?

That dog had a sixth sense when it came to

knowing when I wasn't expecting an attack. Since that first week, he'd gotten me at least three more times. His attacks didn't scare me as much as the first one—I didn't drop the hose and go flying out into mud and dog poop this time. But still . . .

What if that pup turned out to be like Gabe? There never was a meaner, sneakier, nastier dog in the whole world.

So when it came to taking care of the puppies, I left that pretty much to Grandma. And I kept my distance.

Well . . . for a couple of days, anyway.

Since there were seven pups, the puppy poop piled up pretty fast.

After church on Sunday, we all went to Grandma's for dinner. We ate, sat around and visited, watched TV for a while, and waited for Grandpa and Daddy to wake up from their naps. When they started to stir, Grandma said we probably needed to move the puppy pen.

She wouldn't let Grandpa come, because he still wasn't supposed to lift stuff. He grumped a little, but sat in his chair on the porch. Grandma,

Daddy, Mama, and I got at the four corners of the chain-link pen and lifted.

"Careful," Grandpa called. "Raise it too high, and the puppies will get out. Just scoot them along with it as you walk."

Guess Daddy wasn't listening. First thing we knew, there were puppies flying all around the yard. Grandma managed to grab one and tucked it under her arm. Yelling and shouting, she took off after another. Mama and Daddy were calling and whistling for the others, but they were totally ignoring them.

Pointer bird dogs *love* to run. It's just part of their nature. They can't help it.

I started to take off and join the chase, but something bumped my foot. I glanced down.

One of the pups was right beside me. Sitting very straight and proper, he looked up with those blue eyes. When I reached for him, he didn't take off like I expected. He didn't start squirming or trying to lick me like I expected him to, either. Instead, he just kind of nestled his head against my chest, wagged his tail, and looked up at me like I was some kind of yummy doggy treat or something.

Grandma still had only one puppy. She stood in the middle of the yard, so out of breath that her sides were heaving. I trotted to her and handed her the pup.

"I'm still in pretty good shape from soccer camp," I said. "If you hang on to this guy, I'll go help Mama and Daddy catch the others."

Grandma was huffing and puffing so hard that she couldn't answer. She just nodded.

I *was* in good shape from soccer camp, but by the time I got through running down four of the pups, I was ready to drop. What made matters worse was, once we got home, Mama reminded us that the carpet cleaner guy was coming the next day.

I had to straighten my room while Mama and Daddy dusted. Then we stayed up another hour or so moving furniture and taking turns with the vacuum.

Altogether it took about two hours. The house was spotless and I was pooped. I took a quick shower, got my pajamas on, and hopped into bed. The sheets hadn't even settled on top of me when I heard a tap at my door.

"Yes?"

Mama peeked in. "Wanted to let you know that you have the day off tomorrow."

I grinned. Mama smiled.

"Someone has to be here to let the carpet cleaners in, so I told your grandfather that you wouldn't be there to help work the dogs. I'll come and get you after I get off work."

"Okay," I nodded.

Holding on to the doorjamb with one hand, Mama kind of leaned around the corner. "This somebody's e-mail address?" she asked, tapping the corner of my dresser mirror with her finger.

Squinting, I saw the little piece of wrinkled paper she was pointing at. I remember slipping it between the wood and the glass on my mirror—so I wouldn't lose it. But I'd almost forgotten that it was there.

"It's Angie's."

She smiled. "I noticed it when I was dusting in here. Have you written to her?"

"Not yet."

Mama shrugged.

"You're not doing anything tomorrow."

When I didn't say anything, she turned off the light. "Good night, Tom."

" 'Night."

With a smile, I tucked the sheet around my shoulder and nestled my head into my pillow. I did promise Angie that I'd write. And having a day off from working with the dogs would be a restful and fun change.

I could hardly wait.

Chapter 14

Grandpa reached into the coop, grabbed a pigeon, and stuffed him into the small wire box tucked under his arm. He closed the spring-loaded lid and slipped the pin into the latch. The thing kind of reminded me of a hand grenade—what with the pin and all.

"Give me a couple of minutes to plant the box. I'll whistle, and you bring Rex. Keep him on a short lead until you're past the kennel, then let him out to the end of the rope."

Rope wrapped around my hand, and Rex tugging at the other end, I leaned back against one of the barn poles and waited for Grandpa to whistle.

Helping with the dogs was a *whole lot* easier

than e-mailing a girl. I was glad to be back. But as I stood there, leaning against the pole, that stupid letter kept rattling around in my head.

Dear Angie,

That's how I'd started. Then I'd sat there and stared at the monitor for what had seemed like an hour.

When the carpet cleaner guy came, I'd let him in, then gone back to my room . . . and stared at the screen some more.

I don't know how long I sat there when I finally wrote:

I'm fine. How are you?

It should have been simple. I mean, when I was with Angie, talking and laughing with her was easy. It seemed like the most natural and comfortable thing in the world. But trying to write to her . . .

I had probably punched the DELETE button and started over again at least five times. When the carpet cleaner guy left, I came back and stared at the screen. Then Mama got home from work.

And all I'd written was:

Dear Angie,

    I'm fine. How are you?

    I have been helping my grandfather with his dogs. He needs help because he had some kind of operation on his heart and isn't supposed to work too much. So I help him.

    What have you been doing?

    Well, time to go. Bye.

                       Sincerely,

                       Tom

Instead of punching the SEND button, I left the screen on, got up and walked around the room for a minute. Then I looked in each drawer of my dresser—didn't straighten anything—just looked.

Back at the computer, I added:

P.S. I had a great time at Six Flags!

Then I paced around some more, opened my closet, and stared aimlessly in there for a while. I was just about to close the door when I noticed my backpack on the floor. Snatching it up, I reached in and pulled out my list of spelling words. It still brought a smile to my face. I was sure glad Mrs. Nash found them. It made me even happier to think about her being my teacher again, next year.

Throwing the backpack into the closet, I took the spelling words to my desk. For some reason I wanted to keep them, but not in the backpack. I flattened the two pages, folded them neatly, then went to my drawer to hide them behind my undershirts. Seemed like a good hiding place. A place where no one would know they were there but me.

Just as I placed them in the far corner of the drawer, I noticed the writing on the back.

Writing skills. Journal. Letters.

I remembered Mrs. Nash telling us that we would be working more on our writing skills next year, and I'd jotted it on my paper. A sly smile curled my lips. I shot back to the computer.

P.P.S. I got an idea. Why don't we write letters instead of e-mail?

Elbow propped on the desk and chin resting on my fist, I sat and stared at it. When Angie read it, I didn't want it to sound like an assignment, but . . .

I smiled at my computer.

P.P.S. I got an idea. Why don't we write letters instead of e-mail?

Then I added: *It's a little more private.*

Happy, confident, and almost downright proud of myself, I punched SEND.

Grandpa's shrill whistle finally came. Like a rescue, it pulled me back from thinking about the e-mail I'd spent all day yesterday on and into the present.

When Rex and I went around the dairy barn, all of the other dogs barked and bounded against the fence. They wanted out, too.

On the far side of the barn was a big pasture. The way it was mowed made it look like a giant checkerboard. Areas of tall grass and weeds were the squares. The clear-cut paths, where we walked, were the borders between them. Grandpa waited for us at the near edge.

When Rex went tearing into the tall grass squares, he yanked on the end of the rope so hard I almost lost my grip. He ran back and forth in big, sweeping arches. Grass bent as he dragged the rope across, only to spring back and wave in the gentle breeze. We let him run for a moment or two, then Grandpa nudged me with his elbow and pointed.

"He's running wild. Give him a little tug."

I nodded. "Rex! Easy!"

When he didn't slow, I yanked the rope. Not hard enough to flip him or even turn him—just hard enough so he'd feel it.

"Rex," I repeated. "Easy!"

He slowed. Instead of racing through the grass squares, he stuck his nose to the ground. Moved slow and steady. Sniffing all around each square thoroughly, before he raced across the mowed part to a different patch of tall grass and weeds.

A little over midway through the big pasture, Rex charged past a square, and was almost to another one when he turned.

He didn't really turn. It was like something grabbed his nose and turned him. His nose stopped. Then his front legs turned and stopped. Then his hind end slipped in the short grass, until I thought he was going to fall over. Throwing dust and grass clippings in the air, his rump slid to a stop—in a straight line with his nose and front end.

"Good boy!" Grandpa shouted. "*Eeeasy.* Easy, Rex."

The dog stayed, totally frozen, as we walked up slowly behind him. His head didn't move. His tail didn't move. But the closer we got, I could see the muscles in his shoulders and hips quivering.

"Easy," I ordered, sliding my hand up the rope and tightening my grip. "*Eeeasy.*"

Rex lunged. I yanked.

"Rex! Hold!" Grandpa barked.

Again Rex froze. He was still trembling, though.

Grandpa stepped up beside him. He reached out a hand and ran it down Rex's back and tail. Rex didn't move.

"Good point." Grandpa smiled. "Soon as I pull the pin, let him go."

He stepped in front of Rex. Pulling the starter

pistol from the holster, he swept his foot back and forth through the tall grass. At last I could see his foot poised above the metal footpad where he had attached the cord from the pin. He stomped on it. The spring clicked and the wire box popped open. The pigeon, feathers flying as his wings knocked against the sides, burst from the box and flew off.

Rex charged after him. Grandpa fired the pistol a couple of times. It made a loud sound, but smoke from the blanks was the only thing that came out.

We let Rex chase after the bird a few seconds, then Grandpa nodded for me to call him back.

"Rex!" I yelled. "Rex! In!"

The pigeon was already high in the air. While Rex came trotting back to me, the bird circled a couple of times. Once he had his bearings, he flew back to the coop in the barn. Grandpa and I both patted and praised Rex when he came, wagging his tail and his whole rear end.

We put Rex into his pen and repeated the same thing with Sis. Only Grandpa hid the box in a different part of the checkerboard pasture. We were just taking her back when Grandma flung open the front screen door.

"Food's getting cold," she called. "You two quit messin' with those dogs and get in here."

After dinner, Grandma decided Grandpa needed to rest. He fussed a little, but finally settled down on the couch. I flipped through the TV channels, but there was nothing worth watching.

Grandma must have heard me clicking through the soap operas and talk shows. Dish towel in hand, she peeked around the corner from the kitchen.

"Why don't you go play with the pups?" She smiled.

I smiled back and took off like a shot.

Chapter 15

I stopped at the edge of the barn. Six of the pups were piled up—all curled around and flopped across one another—sleeping in the shade. But just like I expected, one pup stood with his paws on the gate, wagging his tail. I hadn't made a sound. Still, somehow he knew I was coming.

When I'd asked Grandpa about naming the puppies, he told me that their new owners would name them. He and I would just call them each Pup.

I named him Tad. I just didn't tell Grandpa.

It was really cool the way I came up with his name, too. I used the initials: *Thomas* and *Angie Danfield*. But if anybody ever asked, I was covered. That's because my middle name is Andrew—so

I could just tell them I used the initials for *my* name, and nobody would ever know.

"Hi, Tad," I whispered. "How you doing, boy?"

When he heard me, his ears perked high. His tail whipped so hard, I was afraid he was going to knock his hind feet clean out from under himself.

Quiet as I could, so as not to wake the other puppies, I opened the latch and let him out. He shot past me, ran a wide circle around the pen, then came back to jump up and put his paws on my leg. I petted him. He wiggled all over, then took off again.

Pointers *love* to run.

A jet took off from the airport. The sound still made my neck scrunch down between my shoulders, but just a tiny bit. I was so used to the sound, I hardly heard it anymore. The puppies didn't stir. Tad didn't seem to notice, either. While he made another circle, I moved away from the pen.

There was a little clearing, near the creek. An enormous stump stood in the middle, just about the right height for sitting.

Perching on that stump gave me a pretty good

view. I could keep an eye on Tad, no matter where he went.

Not that I really needed to.

Tad could run like a streak of lightning. He could cover more ground and cover it faster than any of the other pups. But he always managed to keep me in sight. And he always circled in, sort of like touching base. He'd run to me, get a pet, then go racing off to explore someplace else.

Sure enough, my bottom had barely touched the stump, when he came racing back. Standing on his hind legs, he put one paw on the log beside me. The other paw patted my leg, as if he were tapping me on the shoulder—saying something like:

"I'm here, Tom. Say hello, so I can go run some more."

I reached down with both hands, wobbled his head between my palms, then scratched behind his ears. He gave my wrist a quick lick, then shot off down the slope to go check out the creek.

When Tad came back, panting and tongue hanging out of his mouth, I picked him up. He lay across my lap for a while—head and front paws draped over my left leg, rump and hind legs dangling off my right. After he rested a couple of minutes, he sat up so he could lean his head against my chest.

"I got another letter from Angie, yesterday," I told him. Tad leaned away so he could look up at me. "That's the second she's sent since I e-mailed her. I should probably write her again, but I haven't. So then today—here comes a *third* letter from her."

Tad arched his ears and tilted his head to the side.

"The first letter she sent was a little bit scary. She told me she thought it was 'really romantic' to write letters instead of e-mails. I thought I was in BIG trouble. You know . . . she'd get all mushy and stuff like that. But I think she's okay now. In this letter she told me she's taking dance and playing on a girls' soccer team. She said soccer doesn't last much past the end of September in Minnesota, because of the snow. So when soccer season's over, she's supposed to take piano." One of Tad's ears drooped, but the other stayed up.

"Then she told me about her dog, Lady. She

was a cocker spaniel. She was seventeen years old. Angie said she was really sick, and last week, she got so bad she couldn't even get up. They had to take her to the vet and have her put to sleep.

"It was really sad. You know . . . the way she talked about how it made her feel. I'd write her back, only I don't know what to say."

When I glanced down, Tad wasn't listening anymore. He was draped across my lap, leaning forward to sniff a big ant who scurried across our stump.

I snuggled him again, then took him back to the pen with the others. They were awake, so—careful where I stepped—I managed to fight them away from the gate and get inside.

All of them wanted to be petted. They wiggled and squirmed and went crazy when I picked them up, and tousled their fur. As soon as I put them on the ground, they wagged and bounced against my leg so I'd pick them up again. I couldn't help laughing and smiling at their antics.

Sure that I'd given each of them some attention, I picked Tad up and petted him a minute, then reached for the gate latch.

"See you tomorrow, pups," I said, putting Tad on the ground and ruffling his head and ears. "Be a good puppy, Tad."

"Tom."

Grandpa's voice made me jump. I turned and spotted him standing near the side of the barn. He pointed at the pen.

"Before you come out, bring two of those pups over here. They're old enough to start staking 'em out."

Staking 'em out? I repeated inside my head. *Sounds like some kind of torture technique.*

"What are we doing?"

"Staking 'em out," he repeated. "Teaching them not to fight a collar and leash. Bring 'em, two at a time. I'll show you."

It was downright challenging to hold two puppies, fight the other five back, and latch the gate—all at the same time. Somehow I managed.

One pup tucked under each arm, I found Grandpa. He was inside the barn, standing in front of a long board with big nails hammered halfway into it. A bunch of dog collars hung from the nails. He found one for each pup and fastened them securely around their necks. Then he took one pup and motioned me to follow with the other.

Outside the barn, the side closest to the house, was a big log chain. Its links were bigger around than my thumb. About ten feet long, it was held down at both ends with big iron stakes. Smaller chains, with clips, lay on the ground at intervals along the big log chain. Grandpa clipped his puppy's collar to the first chain. Then he took my pup and clipped him next in line.

"Go get two more."

Glancing over my shoulder, the way the pups looked, made me cringe. The two that were already there were throwing a regular fit. They leaped against the chain. They cried. They bit at the smaller chain. They jerked and hit the end of it, flipped themselves clear over, and whimpered and whined when they couldn't follow me.

When I left Tad, he didn't fight the chain or flip himself over. He just looked at me with those big blue eyes. A sad, pleading look that seemed to say: "I like you. Why are you doing this to me? What did I do wrong?"

I felt like a total jerk!

Chapter 16

About thirty minutes later, after Grandpa and I had worked with another of the older dogs, we went back for the puppies. At the edge of the barn, he held out an arm to stop me. Together, we leaned forward.

All seven of the pups were calm as could be. Three were lying down. One stood, watching toward the house. Tad and the last two sat on their haunches. All seemed alert and watchful, but none were chewing on the chain or struggling to get free.

Then Tad must have sensed that I was nearby. He sprang to his feet, looked all around, then started lunging at the chain again. When he jerked, all the others jumped up and started barking and twisting around.

Grandpa and I stepped back.

"Next time we stake 'em out, they'll still fight the chain," Grandpa explained. "But not as much. The following time, hardly any at all. After that they're ready to put on a collar and lead. Using the chain is safer, too. No leash to get tangled up in, and nobody yanking on the other end to scare them.

"Dogs are pretty bright animals. They learn real quick that once they quit pulling and fight-ing—you know, keep a little slack on the collar—it isn't all that bad. That way we can work them on birds without hurting them. And when the new owners come next week, to pick out their pup, they'll be ready to go home with them."

"New owners?"

"Yeah," Grandpa answered, with a jerk of his head. "Let's go put them back in the pen."

"What new owners?" I asked, suddenly stop-ping at the end of the log chain.

"Well, Jeb Owens is coming Monday. He gets the pick of the litter. Then there's a fella from Weatherford, Texas, and another hunter from Tulsa who told me he wanted one of Angie's pups when she had another litter. They should be here Tuesday or Wednesday."

Grandpa took one of the pups off the chain and handed her to me. For some reason, I couldn't follow. I just stood there, holding the puppy in my arms, with my mouth open. He had to walk back to hand me the second pup.

"Who's Jeb Owens?" I asked.

"His dog, Willie, is the sire. You know, the pups' father. I think Willie's real name is something like Sir Lester Fonsworth of Wilstershire— or some such highfalutin name. Bloodline goes clear back to England. Field Dog Trials champion two years running, and National Open champion about three years back. Jeb just calls him Willie. Good dog, but a little too high-strung for me. That's why we decided to cross him with Angie."

"You mean he can come and pick any puppy he wants?"

Grandpa tucked a second pup under his arm, and motioned me to follow.

"That's the way it's done. Since his dog is the sire, he either gets a breeding fee, or his pick of the litter. I'm glad Jeb went for the pup. Last time

I checked, Willie's breeding fee was somewhere in the neighborhood of five thousand dollars. Even with our insurance—after paying for my open-heart surgery, your grandmother and I couldn't afford that kind of a fee."

Grandpa opened the gate, just wide enough so I could stuff my two puppies in, but not enough so the other two could get out. After I crammed them through the opening, I sprang to my feet and sprinted back to the log chain.

By the time Grandpa latched the gate and turned, I already had Tad's collar off. I held him in my arms. He rubbed his head against my chest.

It's always hot in August. That's why I couldn't quite figure why my teeth were chattering, and why my arms and legs shook like leaves trying to escape a fall tree. Tad just cuddled closer. I clamped my lips between my teeth to keep them from rattling inside my head.

"Grandpa. I was just wondering . . . I just thought that . . . that maybe I could . . . maybe . . ."

He stopped right in front of me. When I looked at his face, I couldn't quite tell what I saw.

Grandpa's eyes were gentle and loving. His

lips curled to a caring and understanding smile. But the set of his chin and jaw took all the joy from that smile. They were stiff, hard, and unmoveable as a mountain boulder.

"I know, Tom," he said, his voice barely a whisper. "You want to keep Tad."

My head snapped back.

"How did you . . . ?"

"I've heard you calling him, when you thought I wasn't around. I've seen the way you look at him. And I've seen the way he looks at you."

Grandpa sighed. His chin jutted out once more. Then he took a deep breath.

"Tom, Jeb Owens decided on the pick of the litter. I agreed. I gave my word."

I heard the gulping sound inside my head when I swallowed.

"I could take Tad home. That way he wouldn't be here when the man came."

Grandpa just looked at me.

That look hurt. I wished I hadn't said what I did. Just the thought was dishonest. It was lying and cheating and sneaky, all rolled into one. The second those stupid words came tumbling out, I wished I could grab them and stuff them back inside my mouth.

My mind raced. My eyes darted from Grandpa to Tad and back again.

"Maybe you could talk to him, Grandpa."

He didn't even blink. "Tom, what you're suggesting isn't right. Jeb gets the pick of the litter. You can't tell a fella that, then add: 'You get the pick of the litter, except for this dog, and that dog with the black spots, and that dog over yonder.' It's not right."

I squeezed Tad closer to my chest.

"Okay, maybe *I* could talk to him. If he knew how much I liked that pup—if he could see us together . . . He's probably a nice man, Grandpa. Isn't he? Even if he's not, he couldn't be that mean. He couldn't take a puppy away from . . . maybe . . . maybe we could . . . Grandpa?"

Little puddles formed at the bottom of Grandpa's eyes. Still, his jaw and chin didn't budge. "Jeb Owens is a good and decent man. He's not the kind who would separate a boy and his dog. But Tom, there's always times when not telling the truth, or hedging just a little, looks a whole lot easier. Safer. And there's times when keeping your word or doing what's right—hurts."

He brushed a sleeve against the side of his head. I couldn't tell whether he was wiping the sweat that beaded up on his forehead, or the little drop that raced down his cheek.

"When you get right down to it, Tom, a man doesn't have much in this world that is truly his own. Friends come and go. You can't always depend on them. And there's tons of people who will lie to you. Always somebody trying to cheat you out of something. A fire can burn your house down. Death can take away the people you love." He traced a finger down the center of his chest. I could tell he didn't even realize he was doing it.

"The only thing a man has—the only thing that's really his—is his word. That and his faith in God."

He cleared his throat and took a deep, wheezing breath.

"It hurts me as much as it does you. Maybe even more. I know how much you love that pup— I knew probably even before you knew it yourself. I could see it in both of you.

"But Jeb Owens will get his pick of the litter. All we can do is hope and pray that he won't take—"

"I hate you, Grandpa!" I raged at the top of my lungs. "Jeb Owens may be a nice man. He wouldn't separate a boy and his dog. But *you* would!"

Clutching Tad close to my heart, I ran for the creek.

 Chapter 17

On my hands and knees, I reached into the bottom
of my closet, shoving the soccer ball out of the
way. Quiet, so as not to wake Mama and Daddy,
I moved some shoes aside, felt around, even
shuffled through a pile of my old toys.

Finally I found my backpack.

When Mama bought notebook paper, she always
got the big economy size. At the beginning of
school, then again around January or February, I
filled my notebook. There was always paper left
over. So I kept that on the side of my dresser.

Trouble was, the letter I'd been writing to
Angie used up the last two sheets from my pile. I
had to get my notebook, because there was still
more I needed to tell her.

I set the backpack beside me on the bed and reached in. Digging around, I finally found my notebook. Shoving my backpack aside, I opened the notebook in my lap, picked up my pencil, and . . .

Went totally blank.

I had no idea what I was going to say to Angie next. So, finding the letter, I started reading to see where I'd left off.

Dear Angie,

I was really sorry to hear about Lady. The way you talked about her in your letter I could tell she was a good dog and you loved her a lot. It made me sad to read that your mom and dad had to put her to sleep. She was very sick and it was probably the best thing you could do for her because she doesn't have to suffer now. But I know it hurts.

Until yesterday I didn't know how much it hurts. I told you about helping my grandpa with his dogs. I told you about Angie having puppies too. I remember because it made you mad. One of her pups has blue eyes. He's real smart and as cute as he can be. He is my favorite. I think (no I know) that he likes me too. Only I didn't know until yesterday how much I love him.

I told Angie all about Tad—how he wormed his way into my heart so quick that I didn't even know it was happening. How he always knew I was near, and no matter how far or fast he ran, he always came back to me. I even told her how I got his name. I told her about screaming at my grandpa. And how I took Tad and hid out in the creek and the back pasture for over an hour. And how I thought about running away—at least until that Mr. Owens was gone. And I told her how I was almost twelve and going to be in sixth grade. And how I was getting kind of grown-up because I had already had my first kiss, and I didn't even think about punching her in the nose.

I told her how, instead of acting grown-up, I'd behaved like a little four-year-old, throwing a temper fit because I didn't get my way.

I told Angie about bringing Tad back and handing him to Grandpa. About trying my hardest to make sure he understood how much I loved him, and how scared I was about his surgery, and that

I didn't mean to hurt his feelings. Only I knew I had. And I told Angie how rotten that made me feel inside. And I left off with:

I know Grandpa is right. I know he's doing the right thing. The only thing a man can do. But it

That's where I ran out of paper. So I started writing on the fresh notebook page:

still hurts!
I don't know what I'm going to do next Monday when Mr. Owens comes. I think what I'll do is tell Mama and Daddy I'm sick and stay home. If the man picks Tad, I'll end up crying. And I don't want to do that. So

I stopped a moment and stared up at the ceiling. Then I glanced at the clock. It was five minutes till one. I stared at the paper for a long time before I took my pencil and marked a big *X* over the lines that began "I think" and ended with "So."

I will go help Grandpa with the dogs tomorrow, because I told Grandpa I would. But when the man comes I don't know what I will do. I really don't.

Sorry I made this such a l o n g letter. I hope you don't think I'm crazy for all the dumb stuff I said. I couldn't tell Grandma or Grandpa. I couldn't even tell Mama and Daddy how I'd acted and how it made me feel. But I had to tell somebody, and I thought you would understand.

Yours,
Tom

P.S. Sorry if I didn't spell stuff right. I didn't take the time to check my spelling.
P.P.S. Don't tell anybody how I got Tad's name. Okay?

I folded the paper in thirds, addressed the envelope, and made sure it was sealed. Then I went to bed.

 Chapter 18

Friday morning, Grandpa and I got two of the older dogs from the kennel. While he held them at the side of the barn, he sent me to let some quail out.

The quail box was at the far edge of the pasture. I don't know what I was expecting, the first time we went to get quail, but that box *wasn't* it.

It was just a tall, green, wooden box with a slanted roof on the top, like outhouses I'd seen. Only the door didn't have a new moon shape cut in it like Shrek's outhouse did.

I opened the door just wide enough to stick my head in. The whole floor was full of bobwhite quail. As they scrambled to escape the "monster" who was invading their home, they climbed and fluttered over one another. They stepped in the big water thing on the left wall, near the door. They knocked feed out of the metal trough on the right wall. One even climbed on top of some of the others and ended up falling out the ramp.

The opening for the little ramp was about six inches above the floor on the right wall. When the birds came back to the box, they could find the opening outside, because it was at ground level. They would walk up the ramp, and hop down to the floor. But once inside, they weren't smart enough to get out. That's because the opening inside was above their heads. Quail aren't the brightest animals in the world. Guess they didn't have sense enough to look up.

Reaching in, I caught one and set him behind me on the ground. Three more shot from the opening, raced between my feet, and escaped. I tossed out a couple more, then latched the door.

Quail love to stay together. The ones outside were already calling—whistling—to find their way back to the covey. If the birds were too close to the box, the smell would confuse the dogs. So I walked in a circle around the thing. Two birds flew off toward the creek. I made a wider circle the second and third time. Three more birds flew off—I'd almost stepped on the last one before he burst into the air. Those birds landed near the cedar trees on my right.

The last circle—even wider than the others—got another bird up. Not remembering how many were out, I figured that was good enough, so I jogged back to Grandpa and the dogs.

We spent the morning watching the dogs sniff and run. They pointed, stayed solid as a rock, until Grandpa or I kicked a bird from its hiding place.

I kept as close to Grandpa as I could. We talked about a lot of things. Most I don't remember. But I wanted to be with him—to let him know how much I liked him and cared for him. And even though neither one of us said a word about the little temper fit I'd had, I hoped that being with him would let him know—would help him under-stand—well, how sorry I was.

After lunch, Grandma asked if I wanted to go play with the puppies.

"Not today." I tried to smile. "I think I'll just rest instead."

I tried to sound light and happy. But Tad would have looked at me with his blue eyes and he'd know. He'd be able to tell how scared I was—how much I was hurting. He'd wonder why I didn't hug him and love on him like I always did. It was because I couldn't.

Loving on him and being with him would hurt too much if Mr. Owens took him from me. But there was no way I could make a pup understand.

So I watched TV instead, and waited until Grandpa was ready to go again.

That afternoon, Grandpa and I got two other dogs out of their pens. One was an older pointer named Sid that he was keeping for a friend who was on vacation.

Rex was the other dog. I liked him. Grandpa and I had worked with that pup a lot over the summer. Rex's color and the way his spots were arranged made me think of Tad, only Rex's eyes were dark brown.

Grandpa said we'd work them together because Rex belonged to the same man, and we needed to finish him.

When I asked what "finish him" meant, Grandpa

explained that Rex could point pigeons. He could find quail, and he was good about holding a point—not scaring the birds up before we got there. But since these two would be hunting together come quail season, we needed to make sure Rex was ready—"finished" with his training.

That's what Grandpa told me.

But while he was keeping the dogs on the far side of the barn as I jogged out to let more quail loose, I figured out the real reason.

Same as this morning, watching the dogs work with quail was a whole lot more fun and interesting than working them on pigeons, or training them to "heel" or retrieve. Grandpa thought this would keep my mind off Mr. Owens.

It helped—a little. But not much.

Sid and Rex found the first two birds within just a few seconds of each other. Sid on our left, pointing. Rex frozen solid and pointing another bird on our right.

Grandpa and I went to Rex. He stayed, paw raised and tail frozen like an icicle, until I scared the bird out of a clump of tall grass. Wings fluttering ninety-to-nothing, it burst into the air. Grandpa fired his starter pistol, and let Rex chase after the bird a few seconds before he called him back.

Grandpa was pleased with him.

While Rex was working his way back to us, we went after the bird Sid had found.

An older and smarter dog, Sid didn't race after his. Well, he took a couple of hops toward it when the thing flew. But then he stopped and watched where it landed in the bottom of the creek bed.

He didn't chase it as soon as it hit the ground, though. Instead, nose to the ground, he swept back and forth in front of us—just to make sure there wasn't another bird hiding nearby.

I could tell by the grin on Grandpa's face that he was pleased with him, too.

But when Sid found his bird the second time, Grandpa was *not* pleased.

That's because—just about the time Sid raised his paw and his tail froze straight and stiff—Rex plowed into the back of him.

Both dogs tumbled. Sid yelped and spun to see what had hit him. Rex didn't even slow down. He just climbed over the other dog, and went off chasing the bird that he had just scared up.

"That's what I was afraid of," Grandpa muttered. "Go grab his rope. We'll try something else."

This time I held Rex. Following behind, we waited until Sid found another bird.

"Bring him up slow," Grandpa said. "Right behind Sid. When he's about five feet away, give him a tug and say 'Hold.'"

Rex didn't hold. Even when I tugged the second time, he still kept straining against the collar, trying to find the bird. I could tell by the way his nose flared—how it made that popping sound— that he knew there was a bird there. Instead of stopping, he just kept trying to see it for himself.

The next time, Grandpa followed Sid and me. He didn't have any more success than I did. Rex never so much as looked at the other dog, or slowed to see what he was pointing. When Grandpa finally got him stopped, and loosened his hold on the rope, Rex shot past Sid and scared the bird.

Grandpa threw up his hands. "Guess we're gonna have to do it the hard way, pup." Then to me: "Call 'em in. We'll wait till Monday. Take him out with Old Gabe."

Just the thought of letting Old Gabe out of his pen sent a chill up my back. I didn't say anything, though.

Mama was there when Grandpa and I got back to the house. She told Grandma that we were driving to Spiro to see Daddy's folks, but we'd be out for Sunday dinner. After they were through visiting, we went to clean kennels and feed. I talked Mama into letting me feed the puppies.

Chapter 19

Daddy was already home from work when Mama and I got there.

"Tom." He cleared his throat and pointed to the coffee table. "You got another letter from Angie."

When I turned toward the coffee table, I heard Mama giggle, then she whispered, "Quit that."

I knew better than to glance back. So I picked up my letter and went to my room.

Dear Tom,

I have a new puppy. I haven't thought of a name for him yet. Oh, by the way, he's a boy dog. Maybe I'll name him Tom, because he's so cute and sweet. But I'm not sure.

Lady was an outside dog. We've never had an inside dog, but I talked Mama and Daddy into letting him stay in my room.

Right now he's snuggled next to me, watching me write this letter.

Here's a picture of him.

Yours,
Angie

For a long long time, I sat and stared at the picture. He was a beagle, with big brown eyes and floppy ears. They took the photo with him lying on a couch, and the little guy looked more like a fuzzy lump than a dog. But he *was* cute.

I could tell from the letter that Angie hadn't gotten *my* last letter. The way she wrote, I could tell she was happy. I could tell from looking at the picture that the little beagle puppy was happy, too.

And I was glad for her.

But it also hurt. I couldn't keep from thinking about Tad. How maybe he could sit on my bed when I wrote her the next time. How we could run and play. How he could nestle his head against my chest when I hugged him.

How—maybe—I'd never see him again.

I stuffed the letter back in the envelope and put it with the others, in my drawer. Then I went outside.

The patio had a big aluminum awning over it. I sat in one of the wicker chairs. Leaning forward, I rested my elbows on my knees, my chin in my hand. For a long time, I sat staring out at our backyard.

It was a small backyard. No, it was tiny. The nearby streets were busy and from the patio, I could hear the rumble of cars and trucks running up and down the freeway, which was only two blocks off.

What if Tad got out? What if . . .

I squished my eyes shut as hard as I could and shook my head, trying to chase the thought away.

Then for the next thirty minutes, I sat there, trying to convince myself how Tad wouldn't be happy here. Bird dogs love to run. Our yard was way too small. They love to hunt. I don't like guns. What would I do with a bird dog, anyway?

And I tried to tell myself that he'd be better off with Mr. Owens.

Then I went to bed.

But I didn't sleep very well.

We left early on Saturday morning, because it was about a three-hour drive to Spiro, where Dad's folks live. I guess with all the flipping and flopping and twisting and turning I'd done last night, I pretty much wore myself out.

I slept most of the way.

Grandma and Grandpa Danfield were quite a bit younger than Mama's mom and dad. After all the hugging and kissing, they sat in the living room and visited. It was pretty boring.

Then Grandpa Danfield got Dad to reset the clock on the VCR, because he still couldn't remember how to do it. We went to eat at a restaurant in Fort Smith. When we got back to the house, they visited some more. I went outside to look at the cows.

But all I could think about was Tad. How he'd love it here. The farm had lots more hills and brush than the land around the kennel. There was room to run—not like our tiny backyard. And Tad would . . .

I bit my bottom lip so hard, it almost brought blood.

Then I went back inside and sat down to listen to them talk, and be totally bored—because it was easier than thinking about Tad.

Monday morning, I still didn't know what I was going to do when Mr. Owens showed up.

Usually Grandpa would be drinking his coffee and waiting for me on the front porch when I arrived. This morning there was no sign of him. I waved bye to Daddy, watched him drive off, then headed to the house to see if Grandpa was sleeping late. Or maybe he was sick again, or . . .

A knot tightened in my stomach. I almost wanted to double over.

Maybe Mr. Owens was already here. Maybe . . .

"Tom! Stop!"

The shout came from near the barn. I spotted Grandpa standing there, waved, and took a couple of steps toward him.

"Tom, stop!" he repeated. "Don't move a muscle. Just stand there."

The urgency in his voice froze me in my tracks.

Suddenly I heard a barking, snarling roar. Hard as he could run, a liver-eared pointer raced toward me.

It was Old Gabe!

Eyes darted to the house—the door—back to the charging dog—then to the safety of the house once more.

If I was fast enough . . . If I ran as hard as I could, I might just make it.

Gabe's lip curled. Long, sharp, yellow teeth caught the morning sun and glistened like daggers.

Chapter 20

My legs wanted to run. It took every bit of courage I could muster to stand.

Snarling and snapping, Gabe slid to a stop, his yellow teeth less than an inch from my leg. I didn't move. I didn't even breathe.

From the corner of my eye, I could see Grandpa walking really fast, carrying something in each hand. I couldn't tell what he had because my eyes were locked on the snarling dog. His hair bristled down his back when he looked up at me.

Maybe Grandpa had a couple of clubs or brooms or something. Maybe he was going to have to beat the dog, to get him off me.

Gabe wagged his tail. But a deep, nasty growl came from behind those up-curled lips, from someplace down deep in his throat.

I needed to swallow, but I couldn't even do that.

"Here," Grandpa said, handing whatever he had in one hand out to me. "Take it slow and easy, then hold it down at your side, like I'm holding mine."

Without looking, I slowly raised my hand. Grandpa put something in it. And even more slowly, I began to lower it to my side.

It was a shotgun, well, not really a shotgun. It was made entirely of wood.

Gabe sniffed my leg. He raised his head and sniffed the wooden shotgun.

"Come on, Gabe." Grandpa's voice was excited and happy. "Let's go find us some birds."

Long, pointed tail whipping the air, Gabe took one hop toward him. He sniffed Grandpa. He sniffed the shotgun that dangled at his side, then . . .

Gabe took off for the far side of the barn.

I don't know what surprised me more—the fact that Gabe *didn't* bite me, or the fact that, for an old dog, he bounded off hopping and as excited as a little puppy.

The air whooshed from my lungs and I gasped

for another breath. Grandpa let out a blast of air that flew up his forehead. It didn't wiggle the hair on his head, because he didn't have any. But I could see the wild, bristly, burly hairs that stuck out on his eyebrows jiggle.

"Craziest old dog I ever saw in my life," he said. "Huntingest old dog I ever saw, too. Long as he thinks we're hunting birds, that's all he cares about. Come on."

Still breathing heavy, I followed Grandpa toward the barn.

"What is this?" I asked, looking at the wooden shotgun.

"My grandfather carved that for my dad, when he was ten years old. Dad played with it a bunch. Reckon that's why the trigger is broken off. Dad waited until I was twenty-one before he passed it down to me. Guess he figured if I played with it, I'd break the hammers off. When you come of age, I'll pass it to you. Try to take good care of it. It's hand-carved from solid black walnut. Thing's kind of a family heirloom. But today, it's mostly for Old Gabe. Like I said—long as he thinks we're hunting, he won't bother you."

I couldn't help but marvel at the thing. When he first handed it to me, I thought it was a toy gun. The more I studied it, the more it looked like a work of art. Its barrels were perfectly smooth, almost like the steel on a real gun. The hand rest and where it was connected to the stock were intricately checkered, just like Grandpa's shotgun. There were even designs carved onto the breech. A picture of a deer in the forest on one side, a flying pheasant on the other.

I was so busy looking at it, I bumped right into Grandpa.

"It's not real," he said, glancing over his shoulder. "But real or not, always treat any gun like it's loaded. Keep it pointed away from any other hunters and dogs. Put it down when you cross a fence. All that stuff. Just like it's real."

"Yes, sir."

Sid and Rex were tied to the fence. Grandpa leaned to loosen one of the lead ropes, then suddenly straightened.

He looked toward the house.

My breath caught. He stood real straight, stretching his neck as if looking at . . .

Suddenly my stomach tightened. A knot came into my throat that I couldn't swallow.

I couldn't look.

What if Mr. Owens's car was there?

What if he was ready to pick his dog?

Tad was the best dog of the whole litter. I didn't know much about bird dogs, but even I could tell that.

What if Mr. Owens chose . . .

Eyes cast down—frozen to the dirt—I walked to the fence, untied Sid's rope, wrapped it around my hand, and ever so slowly raised my eyes toward the driveway.

Grandpa must have noticed. He turned and smiled at me.

"Thought I heard a car drive up. Must have been a private plane, or something, taking off from the airport."

My sigh came clear from my knees. It raced around my stomach, up through my chest, and came wheezing out my throat.

I thought I heard Grandpa sigh, too. Only his wasn't nearly as deep or desperate. "Let's see if these dogs can find some birds."

Chapter 21

While we walked behind the dogs, Grandpa told me that he had already let some quail out. He had tied Sid and Rex by the barn, and was just getting ready to put a collar on Old Gabe, when Daddy and I drove up.

From the time we left the barn until we got to the pasture where the dogs were hunting, he must have apologized about ten times for not having Gabe under control.

The dogs were fun to watch. Sniffing and racing back and forth in front of us, they hunted and searched every inch of the pasture.

"Most of the quail landed along the creek," Grandpa told me. "We'll let 'em hunt up here a couple more minutes. Get a little of the running out of Rex's system. Then we'll head down there."

When we turned, the dogs stayed in front of us. Gabe went to the far side of the creek. Sid and Rex stayed on our side.

Rex was the first to find a bird. He was in some tall grass, and all I could see was his tail whipping back and forth. Then, suddenly, the tail froze in mid-swing. Stood straight and stiff.

"Got one," Grandpa said.

I nudged his arm when I saw Sid.

"Looks like Sid's found one, too."

Stopping, Grandpa frowned and shook his head.

"Nope. That's an honor."

"Huh?"

"He's pointing Rex. Honoring the other dog's point. See how his head's up, not down like he's looking at something in the grass. And if you'll look at his eyes, they're pointed straight at Rex."

Studying them for a moment, I remember Grandpa talking about honoring before. I kind of had an idea what he meant, but I didn't really understand—not until I saw it with my own eyes.

When we kicked the bird up, Grandpa fired. The shotgun was a lot louder than the starter pistol. It made me jump, but just a little.

"You miss on purpose?" I teased.

"Yeah," Grandpa admitted. "But I'll have to bring one or two down before too long. Otherwise, the dogs start getting frustrated or discouraged."

The quail were fun to watch, the way they ran and darted around, the way they flew, beating their wings so fast I couldn't see. I didn't like the thought of Grandpa shooting one of the cute little things. But I understood.

Rex found the second bird, too.

Just like before, Sid stopped and pointed.

"Honor?"

"Honor," Grandpa answered.

Gabe must have figured the huntin' was better on our side of the creek. Before Grandpa and I reached Rex, Gabe came leaping over the ridge at the edge of the dry creek bed.

In midair, his eyes flashed. Legs stiffened. Tail didn't wag—it didn't even spin to help balance him. The instant his paws touched the ground, he was frozen—motionless—in a solid point.

"Now that's an honor," Grandpa whispered.

Sid found the next bird. Only Rex went flying right past him and scared it before we could get there.

"Call him in." Grandpa snorted.

"Rex! Come here, boy."

"No," Grandpa said. "Call Sid."

"Sid? He didn't do anything wrong."

"Call him in."

Sid came running. Grandpa put his shotgun down and knelt. He wobbled Sid's head between his hands, petted him, and kept saying, "Good boy. Good boy, Sid." Then he handed me the lead rope and told me to keep him beside us.

Sid didn't understand. He kept pulling at the rope, wanting to find more birds. I didn't understand, either.

Not until Old Gabe found the next bird.

The old dog was making a turn when he locked up. Kind of leaning *way* to one side, it's a wonder he didn't fall over. Sid stopped tugging at the rope in my hand. When I glanced down at him, he wasn't pointing, but he did stop.

When I looked again, Rex was about ten yards

153

behind Old Gabe. He came racing up right on his tail, sidestepped to get around him, and just as he was about to shoot past . . .

Old Gabe pounced.

Roaring and growling and snapping, he lit into that pup like a tornado. He was all over him. Knocked him to the ground. He snarled. Snapped. Bit.

Even when Rex rolled over on his back to expose his tummy—that's what dogs do to show another dog they don't want to fight—Gabe kept right on snarling and snapping at him.

"Aren't you going to stop him, Grandpa?"

Grandpa shook his head. "Gabe's not hurting him. Just talking to him."

Far as I could see, it sure looked like a vicious, mean, and nasty way to talk. But as soon as Gabe let the pup up, Rex raced to us for protection. He hid behind us, kind of peeking around to make sure Gabe wasn't still after him.

Grandpa was right. He had slobbers all over him, but there was no blood. Not so much as a scratch.

The bird Gabe was pointing had flown off, so

154

he went right on about his business, trying to find another. Rex stayed on our heels for only about a minute or so. Then his instincts took over. He couldn't resist trying to find another bird.

"You want me to let Sid go?"

Grandpa shook his head. "Usually takes twice." He sighed. "Hold on to him until Gabe finds another bird."

Sure enough.

After being attacked twice, Rex was a little slower about leaving his hiding place behind Grandpa and me. But when I let Sid loose, he took off, too.

Sid found the next bird. Gabe wasn't far behind. When Sid pointed the bird, Gabe pointed him. I cringed when Rex came flying toward the two dogs. About four feet away, he stopped and pointed Gabe.

Grandpa smiled. "Yep. Twice usually does it."

We hunted a while longer. All three dogs took turns finding birds. And all three dogs took turns honoring.

Once Rex came down on a point. Only it didn't look quite right, because his tail kept wiggling. Gabe stopped, too.

"What's he doing?"

Grandpa let out a little chuckle. "Field mouse or a rabbit. Old Gabe knows it, too. See how he keeps looking at us?"

All of a sudden, Rex pounced. Front paws together, he hopped on a clump of grass. He must have missed, because just a second later he pounced at another clump, then started sniffing around to see where the mouse went.

"Come on, Rex," Grandpa urged. "Find a bird. Birrrd."

"Grandpa, I don't get it. If Gabe knew it was a mouse or a rabbit, why did he honor the point?"

Grandpa shrugged. "It's what he's supposed to do."

"Even if the other dog's wrong?"

"Even if he's wrong. Guess Old Gabe figures that he can't expect the pup to honor *his* point if he doesn't honor the pup's point."

We found about three more birds before Grandpa said he was getting tired, and suggested we go see what Grandma had for dinner.

I hated the walk back to the house. For the

longest time, I was afraid to look. Even when we put Rex and Sid in their pens, I kept my eyes down. Finally I got up enough nerve to glance at the driveway. A smile tugged at the corner of my mouth when I didn't see a car.

Grandpa took the shells out of his shotgun and handed it to me. While he went to put Old Gabe in his pen, I headed for the house. The house with no car parked in the driveway.

I walked around the edge of the barn. I was still smiling when a movement caught my eye.

There was a man in the puppy pen.

He held something in his arms. I took another step before my knees felt weak and began to wobble as if I might fall.

He was holding Tad.

When he saw me, he smiled and nodded. Then he lifted Tad a little higher.

"Fine-lookin' little pup you got here. Don't you think?"

It took two seconds before I could breathe. Another second before I looked him square in the eye and answered:

"He's probably the best one of the whole litter."

Chapter 22

For the life of me, I couldn't believe I had said that. I couldn't understand why.

It's amazing, the thoughts that come, the visions that flash through the mind's eye, in an instant of sheer panic.

I remembered thinking how bad I wanted to SCREAM at that man. "NO!!! He's *my* dog! Put him down! You can't have him!"

I wanted to race to him. Tear Tad from his arms. Run to the creek and hide. Run clear home. Lock Tad inside the house, so the man could never touch him again.

My eyes blinked faster than a quail's wings

beat. Each time I blinked, pictures flashed through my mind.

I could see the car driving away. I could see Tad standing with his paws on the back window, watching me, wondering why he had to leave, wondering why I didn't do anything.

I could see Tad, all alone in a pen with no one to play with, and no one to love him.

Despite all that, all I'd said was:

"He's probably the best one of the whole litter."

Mr. Owens held Tad up, admiring him. A little shudder raced through me. I closed my eyes. And . . .

I could see Grandma, the day we put the puppies in the pen by themselves. See the look of loneliness in her eyes when she petted the little pup, put it down, and said, "I guess it's just part of growing up."

I could see Grandpa—not crying, but with little puddles beneath his eyes—and I could hear his voice when he said, "Keeping your word ain't always easy."

I could see Old Gabe tearing into Rex. And I could see Gabe honoring Rex's point—even when he knew Rex was wrong.

I could see Mrs. Nash. See her standing in front of the room. Hear her say, "You are an honorable young man, Thomas. I should have believed you."

I thought all that. Saw all that. Felt all the hurt. All the worry. All the uncertainty that went with each thought and each vision. And it was all there— like a giant spark that shot from my head to my toes and back again. And . . .

I knew why I answered like I had. I understood. It was the only thing I could do.

I'd had to answer, truthfully, and without hesitation:

"He's probably the best one of the whole litter."

Chapter 23

When I walked to the pen, the man opened the gate and slipped outside. Once he was sure none of the other puppies had escaped, he tucked Tad under his left arm and offered his right hand.

I shook it.

"You must be Andy's grandson."

"Yes, Sir. Tom."

"Pleasure to meet you, Tom. I'm Jeb Owens."

Letting go of my hand, he kind of stepped to one side, moved around me, and held his hand out again. Grandpa was there. He looked worried, but when he took Mr. Owens's hand, he managed a smile.

"Hi, Jeb. How you doin'?"

"Doin' fine, Andy. From the looks of you, a fella wouldn't even know you'd had heart surgery. Lookin' spry as ever. How you feelin'?"

Grandpa patted his chest. "Little sore every now and then, but comin' around. Where's your car? We didn't see it in the drive."

Tad was wiggling and trying to get to me, and Mr. Owens had to hold him with both hands. I moved behind Grandpa, so he couldn't see me.

"Flew down. I mean, what's the sense having your own private jet if you don't never get the thing off the ground? Caught a cab from the airport."

Guy's got his own private jet, wears blue jeans and old boots that look like they've been in a cow lot or something. Mr. Owens wasn't what I had expected at all.

Grandpa motioned toward the house. "We been workin' a couple of dogs. Just headed to the house to see what Beth's got for dinner. Might as well join us."

Mr. Owens shrugged. "Love to, Andy. Problem is . . . well, I'm qualified on instruments—you know, flying the jet without actually seeing the ground, when it's dark or dusty. Only it's been so long since I've done that, I don't want to. Best pick out a pup and head for home, while there's still light."

Grandpa kind of nibbled at his bottom lip. "What were you and Tom talking about when I come up?"

Mr. Owens held Tad up for Grandpa to look at. "Just admiring this pup. He's a good-lookin' dog. Good conformation. I know the bloodlines are excellent. When I asked your grandson what he thought, he told me he was probably the best pup of the litter. What do you think?"

Grandpa shot me a startled look when he glanced over his shoulder. Then he cleared his throat and turned back to Mr. Owens.

"Well . . . ah . . ."

Guess Grandpa was having a little harder time answering than I did.

"Well . . . I reckon he's a good dog. 'Course you never *know* until they been trained."

"Well, what do you *think*?"

Again, Grandpa hesitated. From behind him, I could see his shoulders sag.

"I think the boy's right. I think he's probably the best one of the litter."

The smile stretched clear across Mr. Owens's face. He puffed his chest out.

"That's exactly what I thought."

In that instant, I knew Tad was leaving. It would hurt—not for just a day or two, but for a long time.

But I also knew that it would be okay. The hurt would go away. If I'd lied to him, if I'd so much as hinted how much Tad meant to me . . . well, that would have stayed with me. It might have lasted forever.

"Problem I got, though," Mr. Owens went on, "is Willie's been my prize dog for years. Don't get me wrong. He's still a good stud dog—just not quite as active as he used to be."

"Happens to the best of us," Grandpa whispered, like I couldn't hear.

"Week before last, I flew to Germany and got me a new dog. His bloodlines are good. Sire won best of breed at the International Dog Show in

Zurich last year. The . . ." He paused a moment. Kind of glanced around Grandpa at me. "The . . . ah . . . the dog's *mother* was the National Field Trials champion at Atlanta two years ago. So . . ."

He turned, opened the pen, and set Tad on the ground. All the other puppies tried to bounce against his leg so he'd pet them or play with them like I did. He looked around a moment, then swooped up one of the black-and-whites.

"What I really need is a female. Kinda hard to be a successful dog breeder if all I got is male dogs. It just don't work."

He latched the gate behind him. Held the puppy up and looked her over again, then held his hand out to Grandpa.

"Think I'll take this one. Okay?"

Grandpa shook Mr. Owens's hand so hard, I thought he might yank the man's arm out of its socket.

"Okay."

We'd only gotten about ten feet from the pen when Mr. Owens turned and looked back.

"Tell you what, Andy. How about I buy that male pup from you?"

My eyes almost popped out of my head. I think Grandpa's did, too. He shook his head.

"What do you usually get for a finished dog, Andy, two thousand?"

Grandpa nodded.

"He's just a pup, but I like the looks of him. Don't even know if he can hunt birds or not. But I'll still give you two." Mr. Owens didn't wait before he said, "Nope. Tell you what. I'll double that offer. Four thousand dollars!"

Chapter 24

Dear Angie,
   I got a new puppy. His name is Tad.

               Your friend,
               Tom

P.S. Forget all the dumb things I said in my last letter. Okay?

That's all I wrote.

I didn't tell Angie how Mr. Owens offered Grandpa a whole bunch of money for my pup, and how Grandpa just laughed at him and said he'd have to talk to me—because he had promised that, if Mr. Owens didn't take Tad, Tad was mine.

And I didn't tell her how Mr. Owens's jaw went slack, and his mouth fell open. And how he shook his head and told Grandpa that he had no idea I wanted that dog. Then he shook my hand, and said something about how much courage it must have taken—not to let on until after he made his decision.

And I didn't tell her how sick I felt when I saw him holding one of the pups. And how I wanted to die when I saw that it was Tad.

I didn't tell her about how, when he asked me if I thought Tad was a good dog, I told him Tad was the best dog in the whole litter.

And I never told her about all the feelings, and thoughts, and things that flashed through my mind's eye in those three seconds it took me to answer him.

I didn't tell her that he picked one of the black-and-white girl dogs so he could breed her when she got older. I didn't tell her because I didn't think a boy should be talking to a girl about stuff like that. Not even Angie.

And I didn't tell her how, after Mr. Owens took all of us to eat at a fancy restaurant and we got home and loaded in the car to leave, Grandpa came running out of the house, yelling at us to stop. He had me get out, hugged me, and gave me the hand-carved wooden shotgun that his grand-father had made.

"I told you this would be yours, when you came of age," he said. "I figure you're there."

When he hugged me, he was smiling, but wiping tears from his cheeks at the same time. And I didn't understand why.

I took one last look at the letter.

Dear Angie,
   I got a new puppy. His name is Tad.
                        Your friend,
                        Tom

P.S. Forget all the dumb things I said in my last letter. Okay?

That should do it, I thought. All the important stuff is right there. I folded the letter, stuck it in the envelope, and sealed it. Then, with Tad following and bouncing against the back of my leg, I took it to Mama and asked if she'd mail it for me in the morning.

The light was still on in their bedroom. I tapped at the door.

"Come in," Mama answered.

She was sitting up, reading a book. Daddy was curled up on his side. The light on his side of the bed was off. But when I asked Mama if she'd mail the letter for me, he rolled over and sat up.

"With all that's been going on today, I totally forgot. You have another letter from Angie. It's on the coffee table."

I told them good night, then Tad and I trotted to the living room and got my letter.

Dear Tom,

This letter probably won't reach you until after the man picks his dog. I hope you get to keep Tad. I've been praying for you every night since I got the letter. Mom says we shouldn't ask God for dumb stuff, like toys or candy bars or even pets. But I could tell from your letter that Tad is more than a pet. From your letter I can tell you love him and he loves you. A pet may not be something I'm supposed to pray for, but I think love is.

Just in case, I decided not to name the new puppy Tom. His name is Tad.

I'm kind of like you. I don't know what you should do when that man shows up. But I DO know that you will do the right thing. You are very brave. I decided that when you turned around in the log at Six Flags and made me talk to you. You knew I was kind of mad at you, but you still did it. Most boys wouldn't be brave enough to try.

Write soon so I'll know what happened.

Love,
Angie

I just shook my head.

"I don't get it," I told Tad. "What is it with all this courage stuff?"

When I looked at him and said something, his scrawny tail thumped the bed.

"Courage is like soldiers who have to go to war. Got people shooting at them and trying to kill them. Or courage is firemen who run into burning buildings to save people.

"Or even Danny—that time when he wouldn't let Harry Mottson copy off him during the math test. He knew Harry was gonna get him after school, but he still wouldn't do it. You know—standing up to a bully.

"That kind of stuff is what I always think about when somebody talks about being brave or having courage.

"What do you think?"

Both ears cocked. Thumping his tail on the mattress, Tad just looked at me.

I turned the light out and lay down beside him. He crawled up, wedging himself between my arm and my side. I had to lift my arm. When I did, he crawled higher and laid his head on my chest.

"Now, Angie signing that last letter 'Love, Angie.' *That* scares me. Handling that—if she keeps doing it—that's gonna take real courage."

Tad's tail just thumped louder.

Maybe it was brave. Sometimes maybe just doing what's right—when it's the last thing you want to do—maybe that *is* courage. Just a different kind. Who knows?

I closed my eyes. Said a short prayer to thank God for keeping me and Tad together. And with his head nestled on my chest, and my arm draped over him, Tad and I fell asleep.